THE LADY
OF
THE LAKE

THE LADY OF THE LAKE

R. E. BRACZYK

iUniverse, Inc.
Bloomington

THE LADY OF THE LAKE

FIC BRACZYK

iUniverse books may be ordered through booksellers or by contacting:

iUniverse
1663 Liberty Drive
Bloomington, IN 47403
www.iuniverse.com
1-800-Authors (1-800-288-4677)

ISBN: 978-1-4759-7400-3 (sc)
ISBN: 978-1-4759-7401-0 (e)

Library of Congress Control Number: 2013902496

Printed in the United States of America

iUniverse rev. date: 3/13/13

To the people of South Central New England

Contents

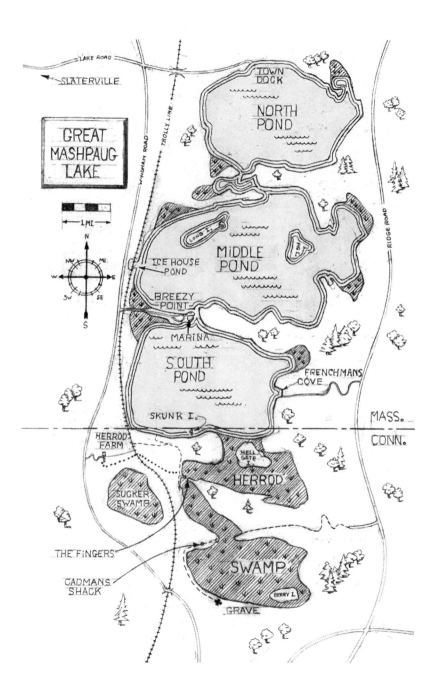

ACKNOWLEDGMENTS

My thanks to all my early readers—Sharyn Finnegan, Bell Adler, Paul Budzynkiewicz, Craig Becker, Lisa Paddock, and my daughters, Maxine and Julia.

Thanks to Brian Emery for his help with the graphics.

Thank you to the people at iUniverse, who made it all as painless as possible.

Most of all, a profound thank-you to my wife, Monica, whose support and encouragement has meant everything.

Chapter 1

Dawnland

An unlined asphalt strip ran due east from the state highway onto a narrow arm of gravel that reached out into Great Mashpaug Lake. At first, Breezy Point Road, as it was known, sloped gently for a hundred yards between unmown fields, and then it crossed an abandoned railbed to level out on the natural isthmus that was as narrow as a causeway. Minutes before sunrise, the cool night air drew billows of fog from the warm lake water, obscuring vast cedar swamps and open ponds to the north and south.

By noon, the August sun would bake the tar blistering hot, but in the minutes before sunrise, fourteen-year-old Ted Samulski could walk barefoot right down the middle of the road. Slim, with sandy hair and dark brown eyes that spoke of his Middle European origins, he was dressed in the jeans, sweatshirt, and sneakers that were his uniform for the season. Except for a bathing suit and Sunday clothes, he made no wardrobe decisions between the last day of school in June and the start of the next school year in early September. At the moment, he had his arms crossed tightly over his chest and was holding a sneaker in each hand. His head was bent in concentration, and his usual energetic stride was subdued. Ted was proceeding with deliberate steps, setting one bare foot down directly in front of the other. The usual feverish flow of his thinking was also in check as he self-consciously rolled his gait—heel-to-toe, heel-to-toe—as if walking some imagined tightrope. He looked neither right nor left; his full attention was focused, through the soles of his feet, into the ground.

As with so many small-town kids, what he knew from school, his own reading, and—most of all—movies served only to inform him that grand and powerful events happen everywhere in the world except here in Slaterville, Massachusetts, in the summer of 1954. What he yearned for was a castle in Wales or Roman ruins to explore. What he was doing at the moment was making the best of what was at hand.

Ted had read somewhere that "Indians" walked in this manner, one foot directly in front of the other, to minimize their tracks. He put that information together with the notion that many modern roads followed old wagon tracks, and that those tracks overlaid Indian trails, which in turn had overlaid ancient game paths. Long before his relatives had come to work in the factories, Nipmuck, Pequot, and Mohawk had known Great Mashpaug Lake as a fishing ground and sacred meeting place. They called their home here in Eastern New England "Dawnland," and rumor had it that there had once been an Indian graveyard out on the point where Ted was now headed. Certainly, he concluded, natives must have passed along this

2

very bottleneck of land in their travels. He could picture them in his mind. What he was trying to do just then was feel with his own naked feet the echoes of those remote footfalls. For the better part of a mile he proceeded in this manner, ignoring the dawn chorus of birds and the sudden glow in the mist as the sun broke the horizon. He worked to screen out any distractions and let in only the faint vibrations that the earth might have preserved. Perhaps the morning light would somehow stimulate things.

Ted was not concerned about traffic. He knew from experience that the wet, foggy air that surrounded him carried sound much better than dry air, and that he would hear a car coming a mile off. In those days, few fishermen bothered to make the trip this far from town, and after all, only one person lived out this way. Then, too, it was Monday. Everybody in Slaterville was at work. He proceeded in his odd fashion past pine groves and stands of hardwoods that grew dense as the peninsula widened. The road eventually began to slope up and came to a fork that wasn't a divergence at all but two ends of a large loop. He chose neither branch. Instead, he headed straight off the pavement out across the large grassy oval in the middle. Most of this open space was dedicated to a sad-looking baseball field that had no baselines or benches and a pitcher's mound that was worn into a shallow pit. A flimsy backstop pulled together from scrap lumber, rough poles, and chicken wire leaned awkwardly behind home plate on his right, at the edge of the road. There had been an attempt to improve it with a coat of green paint, but that only succeeded in making the thing look like some giant dead bug tangled in a web. The dew on the long outfield grass shocked Ted's bare feet, snapping him out of his trance. For a moment, he wondered if he had actually felt anything on his probing walk.

Just beyond the diamond, across the road on his left, was a large, low wooden shed facing north, out onto Middle Pond. Elevated on pilings, with screens all around, the building appeared to hover, so that Ted could see both beneath it and through it to the lake beyond. The outside was painted white, and it had a vast green shingle roof ridged by a thirty-foot-long white sign with black lettering announcing Breezy Point Shore Dining. Both ends of the sign were capped with the familiar red enamel disks advertising Coca-Cola in its trademark script. The interior of the so-called "pavilion" was unfinished pine. The structure was a shell meant only for summer use, rented out for the occasional company picnic, wedding, or clambake.

Ted marched from left field straight across the first-base line and the road, out onto a wide band of grass that seemed to end in sky. He strode right up to the edge, which sagged an inch or two under his weight. The place where he halted was actually a kind of man-made cliff. In front of him, most of the eastern tip of Breezy Point was missing, completely gone except for a band of gravel that described the contour of its original curving shoreline. In the center, where there had once been a hill, there was the opposite of a hill—a hole in the ground that had filled with lake water to become a lagoon. Years earlier, a concrete company from Hartford had mined the high-quality sand deposits. With heavy equipment they had, in a few years, carted away what amounted to a hill fifty feet high and ten times the size of the ball field. They then scooped out the center, forming a sheltered harbor for the docks of a marina.

Vast sand and gravel deposits underlay this whole area along the Massachusetts-Connecticut border. All of New England, together with much of North America, had been subjected to the crushing force of glaciers in the last ice age, and a mile-thick ice sheet had scraped over this very spot for thousands of years. When the glacier began to melt, the outflow of fresh water washed the sand and gravel that had been ground from bedrock. Thick deposits of "washed sand" formed the basin of the lake and were prized for making the best, strongest cement.

Ted was standing on a three-inch mat of tangled roots and humus that was about as thick a covering of topsoil as the area had been able to accumulate in the roughly ten thousand years since the ice. Below his feet, a few pebbles came loose and trickled down a slope some forty feet to an unpaved parking area below. In the years since the excavation, "approaching its angle of repose," as the settling process was called, had produced a sloped face that started three feet behind the edge of the turf. The unsupported carpet of tightly woven roots now had a bit of room to spring like a diving board.

Ted did not think any of these things. He simply bounced once, twice—then vaulted into the disk of the rising sun. His exuberant leap took him five feet out and twenty feet down before he plunged calf-deep into loose, dustless sand. He backpedaled in the little avalanche he had made as a curtain of sand swept along with him to where the larger rocks had tumbled themselves into place along the bottom of the slope. A few quick hops and Ted was on flat ground, headed to the barn-sized building that housed the office, boathouse, and workshop of Breezy Point Marina. On the side facing him, four mullioned windows let light into the workshop. To their right, huge barn doors provided automobile access to the boat bay and its lift. The office was on the opposite side facing out onto Middle Pond. The entire structure was painted white and had the same green shingles as the dining hall above. A wooden walk took Ted around the windowless west wall to a wide deck that ran across half of the building's front. A step down from there, two wharves projected out into the water, serving as docks for the marina's fueling business. Two steps up led to the office door. To the right of that stood a solitary, sentinel-like gas pump, bright orange with a glass globe on top spelling out "Gulf" in dark blue letters against an orange disc. Next to the pump was a reel with a gas hose that could reach out forty feet to the boats.

Ted bounded up the stairs into the smallish office. It had a wide plate-glass window across the front wall, a desk cluttered with papers on the left, and a dusty glass display case on the right containing some faded fishing items and a couple of boxes of candy. A potbellied woodstove occupied the middle of the back wall. At the moment, the stove was completely obscured by the silhouette of a large man dressed all in navy blue. "Mornin', Ted," came a voice in the flat, local accent that tended to drop *r*'s and *g*'s. The owner of the voice wore a mechanic's uniform, pants and shirt, with the words "Breezy Point Marina" stitched in yellow thread over the right breast pocket and "Oscar" over the left.

Ted could smell the mingled odors of clam chowder and coffee. "Mornin', Mr. Morracy," he responded.

Oscar Morracy was heating his breakfast and, at the same time, warming his back against the stove. He was a man in his midforties, with a long soft face, small slit eyes, and a large pulpy nose that just made you think "moose." The elements of his face didn't all come together nicely, so at first glance one could feel a bit uneasy. But when he smiled, his outgoing nature blossomed. He was a single man who didn't care for things domestic. The clam chowder, Ted guessed, was left over from something that had gone on up at the dining hall in the last few days. Ted had known Mr. Morracy to eat a gallon of the stuff three meals a day for a week rather than cook. His clothing came from a uniform service that dropped off a bundle of clean, starched shirts and pants monthly. Mr. Morracy had often joked, "I'd rent ma shoes if I could." What he cared about almost to the point of mania was machines—all things mechanical, in fact. In the last world war, he had served as a machinist's mate, one of the oldest in the navy—and when prodded, he could recount adventures repairing steam turbines in the Pacific during torpedo and kamikaze attacks. He loved the work so much that he stayed on into the Korean War. Repairing outboard motors was now his quieter occupation.

He and his two brothers had inherited the whole peninsula from their father, who—considering it near worthless, bug-ridden real estate—had signed a contract to mine the gravel back in the thirties. It was a concrete company that had built the road and made the area accessible to vehicles. When the war ended and the brothers came home, they divided the land into rough thirds. Russell got the wooded section nearest the state highway, Ken got the middle where the dining hall stood, and Oscar got the large but mostly vacant tip. All three were banking on future development. Russell's hope was that someday people would want to build houses out here; Ken's was that he would grow his business into an actual restaurant; and Oscar's idea was that he could make a living servicing boats. In the still sluggish postwar economy, no one was yet building, bookings at the dining hall were spotty, and the marina was mostly empty.

Mr. Morracy, holding a battered mug and indicating the enamel coffeepot behind him with a nod, said, "Have some." Ted didn't much like coffee, especially black, but it made him feel grown up, so he poured a cup, added extra sugar, and then took a cold clam fritter from a grease-stained paper bag and set it on top of the stove. The fritters, no doubt, came from the same place as the chowder. They were less gummy if you warmed them up. He then sat down in one of four wired-together old Windsor chairs and looked out the open door to the lake, where the sun had broken above the trees. Its warming rays were now striking the water. Mr. Morracy sat down next to him, leaned forward, and propped his elbows on his knees, cradling his cup with both hands to capture its heat. Ted, copying him, did the same.

"Anybuddy out fishin'?" Ted asked.

"Yup," said Mr. Morracy. "Least one, Ed Shields." Though he had seen nothing in all the mist, he could identify an individual by the sound of his outboard motor.

They sat quietly and watched the day brighten. In a few minutes, Mr. Morracy got up, rummaged around on the desk to come up with a dirty spoon, stirred the pot of chowder, licked the spoon clean, and sipped his coffee. Ted put on his shoes and then turned his fritter. Eventually, Mr. Morracy ate his tepid chowder, and Ted munched through most of the fritter.

The sound of chewing was broken by the faint whine of a motor. In the distance, a canoe with a tiny outboard emerged from behind a curtain of fog and caught the sun. The two observers immediately recognized the boat and its owner. "Wally Stevens and his eggbeater," Mr. Morracy remarked, making a joke of the canoe's diminutive motor. Wally's "eggbeater" was, however, doing its job, and the slim boat made a rapid line for the dock. Ted went out. At fifty feet, the motor was cut and the canoe drifted in. Ted caught the gunwale as the feather-light boat nudged the slip. "Mornin', Mr. Stevens," said Ted. "Any luck?"

"Two keepers, then the sun came up and they stopped hitting," was the reply.

Ted was much impressed with Mr. Stevens, a "summer person." Unlike the locals who knew only trolling and bait-fishing, Mr. Stevens was a fly man. His long, supple rod lay across the thwarts of the wooden canoe. A traditional willow creel added a touch that made it all look to Ted like a picture from off the cover of the L. L. Bean catalog. Mr. Stevens had on a new fisherman's vest with large pouchy pockets and patches of sheepskin near the shoulders where he had hooked extra flies. On his head was a brimmed hat with a sheepskin band for more flies. Ted was studying the scene like some museum exhibit when Mr. Stevens lifted his weight onto the dock, saying, "Fill the motor and the can in the bow," and then he stepped off toward the office for a chat with his friend Oscar. Ted tied the painter, turned on the pump, and ran out the hose.

The faint whiff of gasoline over cool damp air pleased Ted. It meant boats and water, fishing and swimming. It was a smell that suggested possibilities. The motor's tank took less than a quart of gas, but filling the big can in front took long enough for Ted's mind to drift from the task. The lake, as he looked out on it, was full of mysteries. He had yet to explore its depths and much of its forty miles of shore. There was nothing here that you could call wilderness, but all of the eastern shore opposite the town of Slaterville, where Ted lived, was undeveloped, and the entire south pond hadn't a single building on it. Swamps fringed the lake in many places. On the southern margin, vast wetlands of grassy marshes and stunted trees meandered for miles across the Massachusetts border deep into Connecticut.

As Ted looked out across the quiet lake, he let himself visualize native dugouts gliding silently, silhouetted against the opposite shore, where the woods still grew down to the water's edge. In truth, the original inhabitants would hardly have recognized the place. Early in the last century, Samuel Slater had brought the plans for the power loom from England and started a factory along the Quadic River, where the town named after him was now located. Later, he dammed the natural lake for an additional source of power, raising its level over ten feet. What had been three smaller ponds connected by woodland streams rose to flood forests and farms, creating the current shoreline. Many swamps still had the stumps of the trees killed by that flooding, and stone walls that marked what had once been farmland could be seen beneath the surface in a few places.

What Ted and his exploring buddies Buzzy and Zolly loved most were the swamps, with their weedy channels, twisted trees, and thick brush. Large areas that were neither open water nor solid land were difficult to penetrate and therefore intriguing. These were the places where twilight arrived early and were the last refuges for fog and mist. Even in wintertime, when the lake froze solid, the swamps had a feel of danger because their shallow water and hidden springs could create thin spots in the ice that were difficult to detect. They were also full of life. Frogs, turtles, and snakes abounded. Raccoon, muskrats, and opossums were common, and occasionally deer could be startled from their daytime bedding. Less seen but nonetheless present were otters, foxes, lynx, weasels, and fishers. All sorts of birds flew about, and of course the swamps were hatcheries for fish: bass, pickerel, pike, blue gill, sunfish, and perch. Bass favored the roots of old tree stumps for building their cloudy green nests. Eel found their way into the many grassy marshes. Dragon and damselflies, with their rustling cellophane wings, flitted about all day. Butterflies and bees paid visits to beds of flowers that would never be picked. Then, of course, there were deerflies and horseflies, in spring there were blackflies, and all summer long, mosquitoes could drive away all but the most determined. For Ted, these wetlands were another backdrop for his imaginings. With them as a setting, it didn't take much to picture the great snake neck and humped back of a brontosaurus browsing water hyacinth in the shallows, like the illustrations in *Life* magazine. On humid summer days, any channel could be imagined into a stagnant tropical backwater with alligators around every turn. Ted had once seen a newsreel of piranhas in a frenzy, stripping a carcass to the bone, and now he and his friends were fascinated by the idea of the savage little fish. He knew that no such tropical creature could exist in a lake that froze over, but when his mind was fired up, he could give himself a morbid thrill simply by reaching into the dark water to pick a pond lily.

The whooshing sound of the gas can topping off brought Ted back to the present. He released the trigger and looked up at the pump gauge, which had rolled to four and a half gallons and $1.38. Inside, he collected $1.50 from Mr. Stevens, returned his change, and sat down to listen. He loved hearing adults talk—not that there was anything of importance being said, but the respect that each man had for the other was appealing, something to be studied. Then, too, Mr. Stevens seemed to have a knack for putting words together in interesting ways. He was a good talker. After a few minutes, Ted's attention made Mr. Morracy self-conscious, so he leaned forward and said, "Check the bilge in the lady, Ted."

A door on the east wall of the office near the desk opened to steep ladderlike steps that dropped down three feet to a walkway, skirting another boat bay inside a shed that was the largest part of the structure. Ted jumped down, purposely slamming his sneakers on the boards. The cavernous space, half-occupied by water, produced a strange echo that he enjoyed. The new lumber construction still gave off a distinct pine-pitch smell that he also liked. There were no windows, and the only light came in through a narrow gap at the bottom edge of the doors that opened to Middle Pond. It glimmered off the surface of the water and reflected up from the bottom to give the whole interior space a limpid, upside-down illumination. Ted thought of it as a grotto he had seen on a postcard from Italy or, better yet, as the lair of some sea monster. Bobbing slowly in front of him, a large dark shape tugging at its lines reinforced the latter notion.

Twenty-seven feet of mahogany and chrome, the *Lady of the Lake* was a streamlined inboard speedboat built in the twenties by the Penn Yan Boat Company. It was the largest such boat on the lake—the largest, in fact, that anyone had ever heard of. From her sharp chrome bow cap, the sides arched out like a plow to cut and turn the waves. In two twisting slabs of rich red-brown wood, they swept backward to come vertical at amidships and then actually curved over in the opposite direction to fuse seamlessly with the deck at the stern. The winding arcs were a marvel of woodworking and had a live, serpentine grace. The boat was also luxurious. She could easily carry fourteen people in soft red leather seats, and her thundering 250-horsepower engine could, with startling quickness, have the craft skimming along at over forty miles an hour. Fully loaded, she produced a wake that brought children scurrying to the shore just to catch the waves. Mr. Morracy had gotten the boat as settlement for storage and maintenance costs when an extravagant local businessman had gone broke. In truth, a large boat like this was a bit of a white elephant and expensive to keep. Varnish and solid wood deteriorated if kept in the water year-round, so part of the reason for the rail hoist that was built into the heavy rafters overhead was to lift the leviathan out for winter storage.

Ted walked around to the bow and sighted down along the keel line, his favorite view. The symmetry from this angle made it easy to see a face—in Ted's mind, a reptilian face. The windshield—two arched sheets of safety glass, angled back slightly in chrome frames—was obviously a pair of eyes. The decking over the bow in front of it was inlaid with stripes of pale wood and bulged slightly across the beam as if pushed up from inside by a life force. Something about that swelling and the stripes reminded Ted of a blue whale. Two large chrome rope guides on either side were easy to see as flared nostrils.

The overhanging bow and its reflection off the water created an upper and lower jaw that defined a gaping maw big enough to swallow three people in a gulp. Ted loved this boat. It was so outrageously different from everything else in his drab hometown. Like all really good things, it came from someplace else, someplace where things really happened.

He continued around to the port side, jumped in, and heaved opened the big doors over the engine. Two inches of water sloshed lazily back and forth just beneath the motor mounts. Clearly, Mr. Morracy had been out on Sunday evening. A bit overpowered, the engine produced so much torque that it strained the hull and, over the years, created several small leaks. A recurring problem appeared where the driveshaft and waterproof bushing went through a bulkhead on its path underwater to the massive bronze prop. Not wanting to start up the built-in bilge pump, Ted retrieved the hand version from where it hung on a nail, dipped it in the lake to prime the sucker washer, climbed onto the deck, and began to work the handle up and down like the shaft of a plunger. In a few minutes, the pump was slurping air, so he finished the job with a hand bailer. Sure enough, a slow steady drip was coming from the usual spot. The problem couldn't be fixed properly until the boat was out of the water for the winter, so the temporary solution was to pack the gap with oakum. He located the ball of thick waxy twine and began forcing it into the void with a rusty screwdriver. About two feet got packed in before the dripping stopped. Good, that would hold until next time. He then checked the gas with a measuring stick and pulled in the hose to top off the tanks (it had two). By then, Mr. Stevens's boat had buzzed off into the still-brightening morning, so Ted went directly to his routine of cleaning the shop. His work schedule was: Saturday and Sunday, pump gas and deal with customers; Monday, pump gas and clean up.

The heart of the marina's business was Mr. Morracy's talent as a mechanic. As indifferent as he could be about his dress or his food, he was particular about his tools. His example of an organized workplace was something Ted admired and carefully studied. The consequence was that the shop needed only a bit of putting away and straightening up. Ted then swept and carried the trash out to the fire barrel.

As the morning lengthened, one other customer came in for a gas fill-up, and the Snap-on tools salesman who always talked too much dropped by. Just after their lunch of clam chowder, potato chips, and candy bars, Ted was watching Mr. Morracy disassemble a carburetor, carefully setting its parts out on a clean rag, when they heard the harmony of two large outboards approaching. Ted skipped into the office to see a pair of gleaming new lap-sided outboards from the big marina up on North Pond skimming toward them across Middle Pond. Standing as he drove the lead boat was Lou Town, the owner of Slater Lake Marine. There were two other men in an identical craft just behind. At full throttle, Mr. Town skimmed past their dock so close that Ted could hear the pennant on the bow of his boat snapping and cracking with the wind. Mr. Town then turned a sharp, sliding circle, cut the motor, and surfed up to the dock on the swell of water that lifted the boat from behind. It was show-off driving.

"Mornin', Ted," said Mr. Town as his boat squeaked into the bumpers. "Got your divin' stuff here?" he added quickly.

"Yes," Ted answered.

Mr. Morracy came up from behind. "Mornin', Louie," he said. "What's up?"

"Mornin', Oska. Could I borrow Ted here for an hour or two? Seems yesterday Whit Duffy's kid knocked a brand-new Merk 50 right off the transom of that Lyman of his. Hit the wall comin' outa Frenchman's Cove at full speed. Mota carried over into that drop-off just beyond the wall. It's down maybe thirty feet."

They all knew the spot. Without any pause he added, to Ted, "Think you could go down and get a rope on it?" Lou Town was the fast-talking salesman type.

"Sure," said Ted as he glanced back at Mr. Morracy, a questioning look on his face.

"Okay," was his boss's response. "Go ahead."

Ted took off like a starting gun had been fired, springing up the stairs to the office where he kept his swim fins and mask in a gym bag. Jacques Cousteau's book *The Silent World* had recently arrived at the public library and had fired Ted's interest in the sport of diving with a mask, fins, and snorkel—"skin diving." He was one of the first in town to have the gear, and it hadn't taken long for word to get around and for someone to put him to use. Early in the summer, when the water was still cold, a fisherman who had lost a rod and reel overboard gave him two whole dollars to retrieve it. After that, Ted had gotten a few other jobs, such as fitting bolts into a dock support and finding a propeller that had been dropped while replacing a shear pin. Ted's mother got a call from a lady who lost her false teeth at the public beach. He looked but found only a tarnished St. Christopher's medal.

While Ted was getting into his swimsuit, Mr. Morracy took the time to caution Lou Town. "Keep the boy safe now," he intoned like a father. As the powerful outboard motor pushed out a plume of white water to accelerate, he cupped his hands around his mouth and called out, "Be ca'ful, Ted." The boy acknowledged the caution with a wave and a nod, but his youthful enthusiasm had his mind leaping ahead to Frenchman's Cove.

Chapter 2

The Lake Bottom

Clouds of gleaming silvery bubbles swarmed past the lens of Ted's face mask as he plunged into the clear lake water. Just below the surface, he cupped his hand to trap a few as they streamed up, forming an air pocket against his palm; slowly he spread his fingers so that they could squirm through to become bubbles again. It was something you could only see with a diving mask. When he looked above water, the gunwales of the boats towered over him, and the men stood out dark against the brilliant summer sky.

It had taken just minutes for the boats to speed through Breezy Point Narrows out onto South Pond. Another three miles in, on the eastern shore, was the shallow indentation known as Frenchman's Cove. Word had it that some Canadian settler had worked the area more than a hundred years ago, but no one knew much more than that. Obviously, the place had been cleared for fields and homesteaded long before the lake had been dammed. Proof of this was plain to see in a typical New England stone wall that sat eighteen inches below the surface and stretched straight across the mouth of the cove. The squarish line of loosely fitted fieldstones followed a long granite outcropping that had been the original shoreline. Though somewhat tumbled down, the wall still retained its general profile and its significant length. The thought of all the lifting and carrying, all that dead weight moved by hand, always produced a sense of awe in Ted. All over New England such walls traced the boundaries of old farmland, and this one was no different. At either end of the cove, the line of stones emerged from the water and disappeared into the surrounding woods. Under the canopy of leaves, both ends turned a couple of right angles to eventually join up in a rough square enclosing about fifteen acres. There were other sections of wall within this large perimeter, carving up the geometry further. The cove now took up the largest of those spaces, some seven acres. All the rest had been overgrown with trees. A rutted dirt track still came down to the water and was kept open by the occasional fishermen whose vehicles could make the difficult mile-and-a-half journey from the paved road. Several yards from the water, a dry stone foundation and a naked chimney marked the location of what had been a small wooden building long ago rotted or burned away. Beside that a gnarled apple tree overgrown with suckers testified to the building having been a dwelling. In their exploring, Ted and his friends had located a good-sized garbage dump, further proof that the place had been occupied for many years. They dug several old glass bottles from the debris and brought them home as trophies of their expedition to this far side of the lake. Ted's mother grumbled about having to clean his bottle, but it nonetheless went up on their mantle as a proud artifact.

The boats had slowed to cruise parallel to the wall, scouting for signs. Perched on the bow, Ted was the first to spot the whitish scrape marks where a spinning propeller had augured across a stone. Sure enough, this was the point where the water was shallowest. Twenty feet to either side, the wall was deep enough for even a big boat to pass safely, which explained how spoiled rich kid Whitfield Duffy Jr. had passed into the cove in the first place. Just in front of the point of impact, on the open lakeside, a large rock had been knocked completely off the wall and lay on the narrow shelf between its base and a steep drop-off that plunged straight down.

"This is it," called out Mr. Town. He shifted the motor into reverse just enough to halt their forward progress and hold the spot as they turned their attention in the direction indicated by the scrape marks. About forty feet out into open water, a small iridescent slick about the size of a dinner plate drifted on the undulating surface. After a long moment, another shimmering film popped up and spread out. The sunken motor still had some fuel in its lines, and it was slowly "dripping up" to the surface. Ted put on his gear and leaped from the bow, holding his mask firmly to his face while splaying his legs just as Captain Cousteau recommended. After playing with the bubbles, he made a somersault to test his "frog fins" and blew a spout of water out of his snorkel. He then swam over to where the gasoline was rising and peered down into the gloom. Mashpaug Lake water was clean enough to drink, as were all the ponds in the area, but because of the humus that washed in from its forested watershed and many swamps, there was a slight green-brown cast to it. In the distance from his nose to his toes, the tint was negligible, but through thirty feet of water the featureless bottom was impossible to distinguish clearly. He kicked into a surface dive and went down ten feet. Another small glob of the gasoline zipped past, and he was able to trace its origin back to a silvery-gray shape that was obviously the lower drive section of a Mercury outboard motor sitting case-down in the silt.

Back at the surface, he motioned the boats over. They paddled to either side of him, and in the odd, nasal voice of someone wearing a diving mask, he related what he had seen. An anchor was then dropped, and the men began to pass long stout planks across the gunwales from one boat to the other, creating a kind of makeshift catamaran.

While they were busy lashing the planks down, Ted swam back to study the rock face at the cove entrance. There were many such outcroppings in the area, though most were high and dry up on hillsides. This was one of the few that were underwater. From its top edge near the surface, the rock plunged twenty-five feet to the lake bottom. Deeply undercut, its base was lost in shadows. In this silent, dimmed, watery world, it was not hard to imagine something dangerous lurking, and the vastness of this fractured curtain of stone disquieted Ted. He swam back out to the boats.

Viewed from underwater, the two white hulls cast long midday shadows straight down, making it appear as if they were perched atop hazy brown columns rooted somewhere on the bottom. With no horizon or other features to judge by, Ted had to rely on this effect and the comparative size of the boats to estimate the water's depth, which also looked to be about twenty-five feet. With the lashing finished, the two boats now floated as one. Ted checked their position and then worked his way around the outside of Mr. Town's boat so that he could tug the stern line and precisely place the awkward contraption over the motor. A second anchor was dropped. He then dove underwater to come up in the gap framed by the two hulls and the planks. Mr. Town, straddling the planks, passed him the end of a thick hemp rope. The drama of the event was building. Though keenly aware of the reality of the situation, Ted couldn't help but indulge in an image of himself as a diver from the *Calypso,* preparing to raise a cannon from some sunken galleon.

"Loop the rope through the handles on the rear of the cowling, so's it comes up backwa'd. And be ca'ful." Those were the only instructions that Mr. Town gave. Ted had great confidence in his ability and was beginning to resent all these adult cautions. He took three deep breaths, held the last, and kicked into another surface dive. At fifteen feet, he squeezed the nose clip on his mask and blew gently to equalize the pressure in his ears. At twenty feet, hovering just over the motor, he adjusted the pressure again. Avoiding the shaft and bent propeller that pointed directly at him, he grabbed the severed gas line and held himself in position for a moment. The soft mud of the lake bottom had cushioned the heavy motor's fall but had also nearly enveloped it. He put his hand on the driveshaft and shook it to make sure the motor wouldn't roll over on him. He then pulled himself closer, at the same time pushing his arm into the silky muck and feeling his way along until he located the handle on the right side of the cowling. Threading a few feet of rope through stirred up enough of a cloud that it made the remainder of the operation a matter of working blind. He quickly felt his way to the handle on the other side and pulled through enough rope to tie a bowline on the ascending line.

Holding the rope, Ted allowed himself to rise a bit, and he was checking his work when a little voice inside his chest began to speak. Up to this point, he had been consumed with the job, but the imperative for air was now making itself known. He jerked the rope to be sure the knot was centered and let himself drift up, readjusting his ears as he went. As he rose above the cloud of agitated silt, he glimpsed something to the north, out near the limit of visibility, but he had no time to think about it. His full attention was now on air. By the time he broke the surface, the little voice had become large and was screaming, his lungs felt on fire, and his diaphragm was involuntarily pumping in anticipation of a breath. He came up sucking the sweet air like a bellows and was surprised to see "Ski" and Benny, Mr. Town's helpers, in the water a few feet away.

"You was down almost two minutes. We was beginnin' ta worry," sputtered Benny, whose big round head seemed to float like a beach ball on the water. After a while, Ted's breathing got back to normal, and Lou passed him another rope. This dive was easier; gripping the second rope in his teeth, he now could pull himself hand over hand along the first line. At the bottom, two half-hitches at his previous knot secured the second rope, and there was time left over to scan his surroundings more thoroughly. He was surprised to find that he could see farther horizontally across the bottom than from the top down. He surveyed the softly undulating mat of lake mud in the direction of the thing he had glimpsed earlier. In the midground there were a few sparse, spidery plants that got barely enough light to survive down this deep and a few scattered rocks that had their outlines softened under a layer of silt, but there was not much else to see until his eye came to rest on what looked like slim spires poking up in two curving rows. "Dinosaur bones" popped into Ted's mind, but even *his* overactive imagination couldn't sustain that fantastic notion for long. In fact, these ribs seemed to converge at both ends in a way that perfectly described a good-sized boat. They were spiky and black, most likely iron, with the wooden hull rotted away. But what boat? Ted had some knowledge of the history of local boats, and nothing he had ever heard of fit the description. Iron boats were for the ocean. He puzzled on that for a few moments before the tiny voice in his chest began to speak again. He checked the rope and drifted up, reaching the surface this time with his lungs only half on fire.

The three husky men—Ski, Benny, and Mr. Town—began to draw in the ropes as Ted watched from the water at a distance. With the slack taken up and the lift lines taut, the "catamaran" seemed to come solidly into place on the surface. The suction of the mud made the first few inches of the lift especially difficult. The two hulls settled deeper as the men began to pull with force, their bent backs and firmly planted feet locked in static exertion. Seconds passed as they strained without moving. Then, as softly as a sigh, the mud released its hold, and the men straightened up erect, the motor swinging free of the bottom below them. Buoyancy made the next twenty feet the easiest part of the lift. Ted glanced down to see a streaming cloud of mud trailing behind the motor as it rose. At the surface, they tied off the ropes and passed down a small broom for Ted to clean off any residual muck. As he worked away, another cloud swirled around him, and Ted flashed on an image of blood in the water that he had seen in a stinker of a movie called *Shark Hunters*. When he'd completed his task, the others passed a length of pipe through the loop in the rope and, with a man on either side, lifted the green and silver outboard onto the planks between the two boats. Water continued to stream out of the case as Lou Town checked the damage. Except for some sizable scratches, a bent exhaust port, and a thoroughly destroyed prop, the motor was in remarkably good shape. The two heavy screws that had clamped it to the transom of Whit Duffy's boat still gripped a splintered hunk of plywood that had torn free in the impact with the wall. Had it been an older machine, the saying "they don't make 'em like they used to" would no doubt have been spoken. So at least there had been a little good luck in Whit Duffy's reckless bad luck. Shuffling the damaged motor across the planks toward one boat and tipping it onto a pile of packing pads took only a few seconds. The men then unlashed the planks, and soon Ted and Lou Town were clipping the waves back through the narrows to Breezy Point Marina. The second boat with the motor and other paraphernalia brought up the rear at a slower pace. Over the roar of the motor and the wind, Ted took the opportunity to shout out a description of what he had seen on the bottom. Ted could tell Mr. Town's mind was somewhere else, and his only response was a distracted, "I dunno."

Hopping onto the dock, Ted beamed with pride at a job well done. The smoothness of the operation had also pleased Lou Town, who smiled as he counted four one-dollar bills into Ted's hand.

"Ya gonna spoil 'im," Mr. Morracy drawled in a joking tone as he emerged from the office wiping his hands.

"He's a good boy. Did well," responded Lou Town.

Mr. Morracy was filled in on the operation while Ted went in and put on dry clothes. When he came back, Lou's boat was a speck halfway across Middle Pond, and the second boat was lumbering into view around the point. Something was yelled out across the water, but neither of the two onshore could make it out. Thumbs were held up; they all waved and grinned. When that boat became an uninteresting speck in the distance, Ted again brought up the subject of what he had seen on the bottom off Frenchman's Cove.

Mr. Morracy, who knew everything about the lake, said, "Don't know any boats, but ya know, Billy 'Hop' Sesnick went through the ice out there somewhares with a Model T back in the thirties, maybe ya saw that." The story was well-known around town. Wild Man Sesnick—a man so colorful that he had two nicknames—went ice fishing in late winter, driving out onto South Pond in his car. Such a thing was safe when the ice was twelve inches thick, but there had been a thaw. Old Hop blundered onto a thin spot, and the flivver was heavy enough to break through. Luckily for him, the seat cushions floated, and he was able to creep his way to firm ice before the cracked sheet could rebound and seal him in to a cold death. By the time he walked four miles across the windswept ice, his clothes were frozen stiff and he had some frostbite, but as he told the story, "That little bit of whiskey I drunk kept me from freezin' solid." Mr. Morracy, who had heard the story too many times, usually took the opportunity to point out, "More'n likely that same whiskey was what got him into trouble in the first place." Ted didn't think that what he had seen was an old car, but Mr. Morracy wasn't that interested, so he let the subject drop. It was like that sometimes; grown-ups responded without really listening.

The remainder of the afternoon played out like most Mondays. There were a few more gas customers; somebody stopped to inquire about renting dock space next year; the mail came; a motor was dropped off to be worked on; another job was paid for and picked up; and Ed Lynstrom drove up in his truck and asked Mr. Morracy to weld a broken mirror bracket. As they averted their eyes from the flashes of the arc welder, Ted mentioned his plans to camp on Skunk Island in South Pond to Mr. Lynstrom.

With a tone that mocked Ted's sense of adventure, Mr. Lynstrom said, "That's pretty far out in the backwoods. Be ca'ful Theta Herrod don't get ya."

The story about the lady who had either drowned or been murdered by her husband and never found was one that often spiced conversation whenever the south end of the lake was mentioned. Her husband had said she went out berrying. Real mystery came into the tale when her berrying pail was found hanging on its usual peg in the barn. Some said her ghost still walked the marshes on moonlit nights looking for her lost blueberry pail.

"Aw, that's a bunch a nothin'," said Ted. In truth, neither he, Buzzy, nor Zolly would have considered camping on Skunk Island if it hadn't been separated from the mouth of Herrod's Swamp by a stretch of open water.

When things got quiet, Ted raked the gravel in the parking lot. Just about closing time, two fishermen with a small boat on a trailer showed up to use the boat ramp. Ted took them to the office to collect their one dollar and point out the nearby spots where fishing would be good between "now-n-nightfall." After that, Mr. Morracy paid Ted for his three days, locked up, and went over the schedule for the coming week. With Ted's camping plans, Mr. Morracy had his nephew filling in. Burt Morracy was about Ted's age, but not much of a worker—no threat to Ted's position.

"See ya next Sunday then," said Mr. Morracy.

"Yes," replied Ted, "unless we get five days a rain. And, uh ... thanks for lettin' me do that job today."

"That's awright, just you be careful. You're no navy frogman yet, ya know." They laughed at that and said goodnight. Mr. Morracy headed along the shore to where he had a small house on the water's edge below the dining hall. Ted set off for the road, carrying his diving gear.

He hadn't gotten far when a small runabout cruised into the mooring area of the marina. Ted recognized its bright blue paint immediately: Howie Langlois, a classmate from school, out for an evening's spin. Ted hitched a ride back to the town end of the lake. A half hour later, Howie let him off at the dock of the Little Cove Restaurant. From there it was a short walk home.

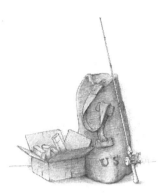

CHAPTER 3

Home

Ted came through the kitchen door just as supper was going on the table. With all the warmth and welcome of a mother who hadn't seen her beloved son since before dawn, his mom said: "Wash up and change those clothes. You stink gas." Ted himself couldn't smell it, and he rarely felt dirty, but he went about his business quickly because he did smell hot dogs and beans, one of his favorites. "Weenies and beanies!" he exclaimed as he slid into place beside his father, hands and face still damp from a hurried job with the washrag.

"That's dumb," said his older sister, Charlotte, who sat across the table from him. "You say that every time."

Ted shot her a look but otherwise let the comment pass unchallenged. For a few minutes, there was silence as the four of them ate. When the edge began to fade from their hunger, conversation flickered on.

"How was your day, dear?" Ted's mother asked his father.

Mr. Samulski—Stan—was a baker, and at the bakery, Monday was jelly-doughnut day. They were a favorite for coffee breaks in the factories and kept well, so on Mondays the bakery made enough to last until Thursday. Mr. Samulski took the floor and began relating an incident with the jelly injector machine. All he had to say was "Mugsy," and his family immediately knew this was going to be funny. George "Mugsy" Magley was a close family friend, and they all loved him. He and his wife often came over for Sunday dinner. With his exaggerated gestures and long expressive face, Mugsy was one of life's natural comics, always good for a laugh.

"So, he's workin' his way through a few trays of empty puffs, fillin' 'em," Mr. Samulski continued, "two at a time, takin' one in each hand, he's pushin' 'em onto the spigots and hittin' the floor switch with his foot. He's got raspberry in the machine. Everything's goin' fine, then somehow, the switch gets stuck on, and the thing begins firing tablespoon-sized blobs of red jelly nonstop. At first, Mugsy tries ta catch 'em in his hands and put 'em back in the hopper, but he can't keep up, so he goes ta the floor ta try ta free the switch. Of course, the machine keeps right on, and now he's gettin' jelly down his back, so he stands up and starts catchin' it in his hat. The hat's fillin' up, just about to burst, and Mugsy's dancin' around, yellin' for help, when Frank gets free from what he's doin' and jumps over ta yank out the plug. Jelly's everywhere, puddles on the floor, and there stands Mugsy, with this mournful puss like Buster Keaton or somebody, lickin' his fingers, and he says, calm as you please, 'Maybe da seeds gut stuck somewhares.'" The family exploded in laughter. It was an image they could all picture.

"What did he do with the jelly in his hat?" asked Ted.

"Put it right back in the machine, freed up the switch, and kept goin'," his father answered with a grin. "But don't tell anybody that."

The opportunity to speak then passed naturally to Mrs. Samulski, who brought things down to earth with the news that old Mrs. Chatterton from across the street had fallen and broken her hip.

"The ambulance was here and everything," said Mrs. Samulski. "They took her to the hospital, but ya know ..." There was not much else to say.

Charlotte then got to report on her babysitting job for a "summer family" from Boston, the McCrerys. They had one of the big old houses on North Pond, and she was much impressed with the way they lived. Everything they had was the best and the most modern. They even had a cook. There was, however, this "fancy" toilet seat in the master bathroom that would shoot a stream of warm water on your backside when you pushed a button, which puzzled her. Everybody at the table agreed that it must be some new thing that "city people" did, but that it was perhaps a bit strange. Mrs. Samulski, who prided herself on keeping the cleanest house in the neighborhood, thought it might not be an altogether bad idea—just not supper-table conversation. And by the way, what was Charlotte doing in the master bathroom?

Ted had been patiently waiting to talk about his day and drew his story out right through dessert and doing the dishes. There were many questions. His mother's were about safety, his father's were on technical things, and Charlotte's were about "all that icky mud." Ted proudly waved his four dollars in her face and pointed out that "the money doesn't have any mud on it." When the dish drainer was being put away, Ted's mother reminded his father: "That wasp nest in the bushes, Stan." Reluctantly, Mr. Samulski set aside his paper and went to retrieve a brown paper grocery bag and flashlight from where they were kept under the sink. Ted followed as his father headed out the front door. It was almost dark and the cool night air was on them as Mr. Samulski parted the outer green of the arborvitae. Ted shined the light to reveal a pale gray paper-wasp nest about the size of a football worked onto the branches roughly five feet off the ground. The wasps were inactive at this temperature, so there was little danger. During the day, however, the nearness of the nest to the walkway and the mailbox made for a potential problem.

"Hate ta do this," his dad muttered with a tone of regret. They went around back to the garden shed to get a pair of gloves, a short stick, pruning shears, and an inch of gasoline in an old coffee can. Back on the front walk with the gloves on and Ted holding the light, it was an easy matter for Mr. Samulski to reach in and plug the exit hole with the stick, and then slowly pour the gas over the nest. As the liquid spread out, it soaked the dry paper of the nest dark, almost black. Ted could hear muffled buzzing from inside. Without much fuss, his father then slipped the grocery bag over the nest and cut the branches that anchored it with the shears. When it came loose he tipped the bag up, rolled the top closed, walked to the fire barrel, tossed it in, and lit a match. With gasoline involved, flames flared like a torch and burnt fiercely for a minute or two. Nothing stirred from the nest. No stream of angry wasps poured out to retaliate, as they always did in cartoons. There was no rattling buzz at his ears, not even the threat of a sting. Ted felt oddly sad to see these fearsome insects that had earned his grudging respect die so easily. As they turned back to the house, his dad took a moment to address the ashes. "Sorry about that, fellas," he said into the embers. To Ted, he said, "I hate ta do stuff like that. They were just tryin' ta make a livin'." Mr. Samulski was always on the side of the workingman.

Inside, Ted's mom was laying out items from her pantry that worked as camp food. With the kitchen table as a staging area and a checklist in hand, she was setting out salt, oil, flour, powdered milk, oatmeal, a can of Spam, macaroni—things like that. She herself loved camping, and her enthusiasm had rubbed off on Ted, even though he thought her a bit too organized. When she had run through her list of food and put all the items in a cardboard box, she turned her attention to sleeping gear. They had an army surplus mummy bag and a jungle hammock. There was a lot of this army gear around after the Second World War and Korea. Every town seemed to have its army-navy store, and everything that the country had produced to fight the Germans, Japanese, and North Koreans—except the guns—was for sale there. Boys loved the stuff because it had the spirit of adventure about it and it made them feel grown up, like their fathers who had served in the war. Most of these surplus items were, however, bulky, difficult to use, and usually damaged in some way.

Ted grudgingly endured his mother's explanation of the clothes she had set out for him, but in the long run he was grateful when all of it was neatly packed away into his dad's old duffel bag and sitting next to the kitchen door, waiting for the morning.

That night, Ted slept the last sleep of his childhood.

Chapter 4

Skunk Island

It had taken nearly three hours to row the length of the lake from its north shore to this extreme southern end on the state line. For Ted and Buzzy, it felt like they had left civilization behind and were now deep in the somber Maine wilderness. Zolly was not yet completely in harmony with their feelings.

"The naughty lady of Shady Lane has the town in a whirl.

The naughty lady of Shady Lane. Me oh, my oh, what a girl.

Bum, bidda, bum bum bum bum—bum, bidda, bum bum bum."

He had belted out the lines from a current Ames Brothers hit for about the hundredth time since before dawn when they had left the town mooring. It was now near nine a.m., and he was wearing the tune very thin. It didn't matter to him that

33

the playful little song about a naughty lady who throws "come hither" glances and never refuses "liquid refreshment" resolved itself by revealing that "she was ooown-leee nine days ooooold." The concept of a lady who was "naughty" and associated with anything "shady" immediately brought the most suggestive interpretation of the words to his fertile adolescent mind. Ted and Buzzy let him go on with his yowling because it spurred him to row with great force. The activity also distracted him, so that he was not paying close attention to where he was going. He got his comeuppance in a moment.

The bow of the sturdy rowboat plowed into the gravel margin of Skunk Island so suddenly that Zolly lost his grip on the oars and tumbled backward onto the gear behind him. The other two laughed gleefully and scrambled over to pull the old tub farther up onto the narrow beach. Their boat belonged to Mr. Sweeny, Buzzy's father, and was typical of the many homemade rowboats on the lake. Each side was a solid plank of pine, eighteen inches wide, that curved forward from the heavy blunt transom to the bow, where they joined in a point. The bottom was simply more boards attached parallel to the beam so that they swelled to fit watertight. A shallow keel supported them underneath. All you could say about the inside was that it had three thwarts and a pair of oarlocks set in the double-thick gunwale. Boats like this had a shallow draft and were good in the swamps, but they were heavy and didn't glide well. Like many of the others, this one had been painted inside and out with leftover gray house paint. Humble in the extreme, this awkward craft was the boys' conveyance to adventure and independence. Now, for a few days, they could live on their own, and every plunge of the heavy oars drew them away from their daily lives hemmed in by adult rules and small-town restrictions. They were all feeling some of the outrageousness that Zolly was expressing with his crude interpretation of "The

Naughty Lady of Shady Lane"—but when he peed off the back of the boat as the others were trying to troll, he went too far and needed a lesson. His friends took advantage of the lull in his high spirits caused by his backward tumble to establish a more serious camp-setting-up mood. He grumbled a bit but soon fell in line, unloading his gear and dragging the boat further up as it lightened. They all loved camping, and the work of setting up their site was a group effort.

Skunk Island was a low gravel dome about an acre in size. Nowhere did it rise more than three feet above the waterline, which was fringed with blueberry bushes. A grove of ancient, lightning-blasted pines occupied the center. It must have once been the top of a small hill connected to the nearby shore, but the new lake level surrounding it defined a rough silhouette that most people thought "looks somethin' like a skunk"—one with its tail raised. The tail (actually a peninsula) was the south end of the island and too narrow to camp on. At the north end, where the head would be, was a large glacial erratic known, not surprisingly, as the Skunk's Nose. In the center of what would be the body, the old pines established the familiar "cathedral" space that was so inviting as a campsite.

A blue jay let out a warning cry, announcing their arrival to the empty island. The place was too small for any large animals. Ted didn't think that even mice could survive out here—there was no way for them to "earn a livin'," as his father might say. In an hour they had cleared a site, pitched Buzzy's heavy three-man sidewall tent, rearranged the rocks of an old fire pit into a serviceable cooking area, gathered wood, and dug a cooler down at the water's edge for the few items that needed to be kept cold—if you could call a water temperature of sixty-eight degrees cold. Finally, they dug a slit trench, strung Ted's jungle hammock to use for storage, and looked around with satisfaction. The little pine grove with the midday sun filtering through the boughs now had a decidedly homey look in their eyes. It would be a good place to return to in the evening.

Lunch was their next order of business. When he had dropped off the three boys on his way to work, Ted's dad had bought them each a bottle of Coke from the vending machine at the town landing. That—along with some slabs of ham, rye bread, and mustard that Ted's mother had packed—was lunch. Through mouthfuls of thick bread, salty meat, and sweet soda, they all agreed that Ted's mom was "okay." Well-fed and reveling in their freedom, the boys had an afternoon bright with possibilities before them. Earlier, Ted had mentioned the curious thing off Frenchman's Cove, and the idea of exploring for sunken anything carried the day.

This odd association would never really tolerate a leader, but Ted often came up with good ideas for things to do. The three were drawn together for negative reasons as much as anything—which is to say, they didn't fit in with groups or cliques at school. In the positive sense, they were building their friendship from a foundation of what they had in common: a yearning for experience and avid curiosity. They were gradually developing the trust that comes from shared experience.

Ted was a fair student, but he hadn't as yet discovered any enthusiasm for classroom work. Sports held no interest for him, and any real attraction to girls was still over the horizon. Except for being a little bookish, he didn't stand out in any particular way among his peers.

Buzzy was a poor student and resisted school. His family life and awkward physique had gotten him off to a bad start as early as the first grade, and things had never improved. Tall, with a small head, narrow shoulders, and wide hips that gave him the general shape of a bowling pin, he had early on been tagged with the nickname "Lard-ass," and that stigma had

followed him everywhere. Persistent taunting had affected his
academic success, and eventually teachers began to treat him as
if he were thick and sluggish. At this point in life, his plan was
to quit school when it was legal at sixteen and go to work. His
single father and grandmother were the ones raising Buzzy; for
reasons left unspoken, there was no Mrs. Sweeny around, and
Mr. Sweeny, a nice though consistently glum man, regularly
consoled himself with drink. The spectacle of his periodic
public drunkenness was deeply humiliating for his son. Buzzy's
grandmother spoke no English, always wore a black kerchief,
kept chickens in the house, and dressed Buzzy with an Old
World sense of frugality that sent him out the door looking
like a well-scrubbed, overly mended fugitive from the charity
store. He was by no means dull-witted or clumsy, and he had a
basically optimistic nature, but in a small New England town
with many even smaller-minded citizens, he was being pushed
to the margins. Circumstances made him an outsider both
figuratively and literally. Having almost no social life, he sought
refuge in the surrounding forests and farms—the outdoors for
an outcast. From the moment he was old enough to go on his
own, he had explored the town and its surroundings. Of the
three, he was the only one who would camp by himself, and
he was by far the most experienced at it. Ted and Zolly relied
on his considerable skill as a cook.

Zolly was another case all together. To begin with, his
full name was Zoltan Dracut, and he spoke with a Hungarian
accent. His family had emigrated when he was eleven, and
though he had light hair and blue eyes, it didn't even take a
full first day in the sixth grade for someone to begin taunting
him with "Hey, Dracula." Unlike Buzzy, Zolly reacted by
giving it right back to his tormentors, and he often landed in
the principal's office. His father held the prestigious job of head
chemist at the Pautuxen Print Works, his mother was a doctor,

and both parents had a snobbish, superior attitude toward the locals that rubbed off on their son. He had an arrogant streak and was the one among them who was most anxious to be initiated into the adult world. To put it bluntly, Zolly could be a pain in the ass, but like everyone, he craved acceptance and friendship, and he was smart enough to tone down his attitude around Ted and Buzzy. Out in the woods, away from social pressures, things got leveled out—simplified—and the three got along. Zolly's mercurial personality was balanced by Buzzy's patient plodding, and Ted found himself somewhere between the two.

With high spirits they pushed off from Skunk Island for the mile-and-a-half row to Frenchman's Cove. Scattered good-weather clouds, no wind, and a lighter boat made it a pleasant sprint compared with the morning's long slog. There was not a single house on all of South Pond. No one was building out this far as yet, and at the moment, there were no other boats. Surrounded by a vast rim of green woodlands capped with a lens of blue sky, they had the entire world to themselves.

Ted had a general sense of the spot they were aiming for, but as they glided into the area, he had to go over the side to reconnoiter. A few shallow dives and he was able to guide the anchor drop to within a few feet of their target. The other two then joined Ted in the water, and they passed the diving mask back and forth for a look. From the surface, even with the mask on, you couldn't see clear to the bottom. So each took a turn diving down a few feet. They all agreed the thing didn't look much like a Model T. It was undoubtedly a boat and quite a large one for the lake: about twenty or twenty-five feet in length, with a beam around nine feet across. From their vantage point directly overhead, they could see that the outline tapered at both bow and stern, like a whaler or a lifeboat.

With only one set of diving gear, they would have to

take turns. Ted went down first. He pulled himself hand over hand along the anchor rope to the port side along the line of protruding ribs. When he reached out to grab one, it disintegrated in a puff of orange dust, leaving a dark black stain on his palm—a sure indication that the ribs were made of iron. Pieces of rotted planking still clung here and there, but the boat was settled deeply into the mud, obscuring most of the hull. What he was seeing were only the tips of its ribs near the gunwale that had completely rotted away. The boat had come to rest in a natural depression that was perhaps the reason fishermen who knew the lake bottom by the obstacles that snagged their hooks hadn't discovered it. A line of boulders several yards to the north and somewhat visible from the surface would have drawn the blame for any such fishing mishaps. The shadow from the rowboat drifted across the wreck, casting contours that revealed a curiously geometric pattern, rather like a tumble of blocks with their edges softened by the enveloping sediment. Ted swam to amidships and gently fanned one protruding mound with his hand. Before visibility became clouded, he was able to see what was clearly the corner of a rough wooden box or crate.

Back in the boat, there was speculation over what they had found. Whatever it might be, there was clearly a lot of it. No one could have stopped Zolly from taking the next turn. After a few experiments and Ted's coaching, he figured out how to equalize the pressure in his ears. "Be careful," Ted found himself saying almost involuntarily as Zolly gulped air for his first dive. But they were all good swimmers, so Zolly got himself to the bottom as easily as Ted had done. The dust that Ted had stirred up was now settled, and the corner of the box stood out. Its spongy, rotted wood was slimy to the touch. What nails there were had mostly rusted away, so Zolly had no difficulty pulling the wood apart with his bare hands. As the blackened slabs crumbled and slid away, a shiny metal surface with a fine decorative pattern flashed before another green cloud obscured things. Zolly swung around and fanned the area by kicking hard with the swim fins, pushing large gusts of clear water downward. Though the effort drove him in the opposite direction, he still had a moment to glimpse a metal box about the size of the old-fashioned cash register that Mr. Morracy used at the marina—but this one had a stout lever arm coming out of its left side.

As Zolly coughed out his description between gulps of air, Ted and Buzzy simultaneously realized what they had. Though neither of them had ever actually seen one before, they recognized that it was a slot machine, a one-armed bandit. They caught Zolly up quickly. From the generation of older uncles and aunts who had come of age during the Roaring Twenties and Prohibition, they had heard stories of moonshine, bootlegging, speakeasies, and illegal gambling. Ted's uncle Steve, in particular, reveled in telling anyone who would listen exaggerated tales of his own misspent youth. Though he was now an upright citizen with a job in the post office, Uncle Steve was full of interesting stories—both firsthand and secondhand—of secret gin joints and hidden gambling dens that popped up like mushrooms, thrived for a short time, and then vanished in a night. Many of the events he related had to do with crossing borders to evade the police in one town or another. In those days, Connecticut had no state police, so getting over that state line was a particularly important gambit in these illegal dashes from the arm of the law. The lake, with its north end deep in Massachusetts and the other over the Connecticut line to the south, must have figured into all this.

As the boys talked, their level of excitement grew. Quickly, however, they exhausted their knowledge of the subject, so pulling up their discovery was the only logical next step. With the end of their second anchor rope in hand, Buzzy approached the sunken slot machine. A dusting of silt had again settled over it, dulling its sheen but leaving its form clearly visible. He had tied a slipknot at the surface, and it was a simple matter to slide it over the lever arm and cinch the knot tight. He then repeated Zolly's maneuver, and holding the rope to keep himself in place, he kicked in all directions with the fins to clear as much of the blanketing silt as he could before letting go and drifting to the surface.

Buzzy had trouble climbing back into the boat, and the others laughed as they pulled him in. He quickly made up for that humiliation by single-handedly pulling up the waterlogged machine. When they felt it thump against the bottom of the boat, it was a fairly simple matter for Ted and Zolly to reach over and haul it up onto the transom. As it balanced there on its side, they studied the blocky machine, water gurgling out through the coin slot. That slot was wide, about the size of the biggest coin they knew, a silver dollar. With great interest, the boys watched as the water level receded behind the little glass window that protected the iconic spinning drums with their bars and cherries and bells. The white enamel surfaces of the drums were now pitted with dots of bright orange rust. When the dripping slowed, the boys tipped the machine upright onto the boat's rear seat. As they did, they heard a sound that stopped them dead.

"Oh my god" was all Ted could manage. He and Zolly just looked at each other.

Buzzy, who was sitting in the bow to keep the boat trim, let his jaw drop. Only a few seconds passed before Zolly grabbed the case and shook it until they heard the unmistakable sound of coins rattling around inside—the sharp tinkling sound of silver coins sliding over each other. There seemed to be quite a few. After that, they found themselves sitting down, blinking in disbelief.

"Treasure, real treasure," muttered Zolly. They couldn't yet know for sure, so they began an inspection. The entire upper case was cast in one piece from a metal alloy that seemed impervious to rust. It had a small door at the back that required some sort of a key, but the bottom, with four severely rusted iron screws, seemed vulnerable. Laying the case on the coiled anchor rope, Ted rammed it with the butt end of an oar a few times to no effect. He then broke the glass, and they tried to shake something out. There was enough large debris inside to block the opening. Not much came out, and the whole machine was just too heavy to shake with any vigor. They looked back across South Pond to the island, where they had left the ax at their campsite. The shore of the cove was much closer, so they pulled up the anchor and rowed in. When they had beached the boat, stern first, Ted and Zolly coordinated a lift. With the metal box balanced over their heads, they agreed on a target, counted to three, and slammed the thing down onto a nearby granite slab with all their might. The case hit on a bottom corner, and the insides shot out as if propelled by explosion. The outer metal box rebounded with a dull, bell-like sound and cartwheeled into the bushes ten feet away. The rusted mechanism with the arm still attached tumbled back toward the water's edge. Between these two big pieces of junk, dozens of tarnished metal discs flew up into the air.

"Oh-ma-god, oh-ma-god, oh-ma-god, oh-ma-god," Ted cried in a rising crescendo as he sank to his knees to pick up one of the gray discs. In a minute, each boy had fistfuls of silver dollars, which they dumped on the same rock that had served as their anvil. They counted forty-one. "Startin' wage at Norman Shoe is seventy cents an hour ... this is a lot a money," said Buzzy earnestly, "over a week's pay."

"Treasure," hissed Zolly, and he plunged his hands into the small pile and then let the coins fall through his fingers. He bit one with his teeth, like Robert Newton in *Blackbeard*, but a silver dollar didn't yield like a soft gold doubloon. He then scrubbed it with sand to confirm that it at least shined. Before they rowed back out, they found several more coins stuck in a long tube inside the rusted mechanism. Though they cleaned up the area by tossing telltale parts into the bushes, they missed one coin.

><del>

Not all of the machines were as ideally oriented as the first, so by four o'clock they had brought up only four more—three that took silver dollars and one that took fifty-cent pieces. Back on shore, however, they improved their technique, finding that they didn't need to use quite as much force as they had on the first machine. So there wasn't as much scurrying about afterward to collect the booty.

Though their enthusiasm didn't flag, being up before dawn began to take its toll, and with the sun still four hand-widths from the horizon, they decided to call it quits for the day. There was no question that they would be back in the morning. Counting the coins again, they found they had $175. The row back was unusually quiet, with each of them lost in his own thoughts. It was all still a shock—a good one to be sure, but the kind of thing that seemed hard to believe the moment they stopped the actual activity of recovery. Each of them needed an occasional glance at the coins balled up in a towel on the rear seat for assurance that this was really happening.

Ted broke the silence. "If we tell anybody about this, they're gonna take it away for sure."

"Remember the John Wayne movie *Reap the Wild Wind*, about the deep-sea divers?" said Zolly. "They found a wreck and got to keep everything."

"In that movie, the wreck was in international waters.

Da ya think the bottom of Mashpaug Lake is international waters?" said Buzzy. They all grinned at the obvious answer to that question.

"Well," said Ted, "let's get our hands on as much as we can first, then we talk. At least we'll be famous for findin' it."

The idea of glory pleased Zolly, and he looked forward to the admiration and acceptance he thought that would bring. Buzzy could think only *Money!* Of the three, his family had the least, and he nudged the bundle several times to feel its solidity. The idea of glory wasn't missed by Ted, but he was just plain curious.

Back at the island, they roused themselves from their thoughts as the necessities of camp life took over. Before they had set out earlier, each had baited and cast off a line set up for bottom fishing. Fortunately, each had caught something for supper: they had a medium-sized bass and two pout, a local type of catfish. Buzzy went to start a fire and began cooking, while Ted cleaned the fish. Zolly took the task of finding a place to hide the coins. Ted didn't mind cleaning bass, but pout were another matter. They were black and ugly, with horns. Their pectoral fins were bony spurs about an inch long, and the dorsal fin began with another spike that popped up as if on a spring. If you weren't careful, they could flip about and stick you—and the wound usually festered. On top of that, they were slimy and couldn't just be gutted and scaled. They had to be skinned. The good part was that they yielded a delicate pink flesh that had few bones. Ted took the fish out to a fallen log that extended into the water and worked for twenty minutes to produce a nice pile of meat. The entrails and heads were thrown out into the lake. They would be gone by morning, eaten in the night by snapping turtles, most likely.

When Ted returned, Buzzy had the fire down to an even

bed of coals and was chopping onions, carrots, and celery on a wide pine board. An old refrigerator shelf over the fire served as a grill.

"Where'd ya get those?" asked Ted, indicating the grill and cutting board. They hadn't come on the boat.

"I hide 'em out here so's I don't hafta bring 'em with me," Buzzy responded.

Obviously, Buzzy did a lot more camping than Ted knew about. He put the fish down on the board as Buzzy began peeling potatoes with a skill that reminded Ted of his mother. The scraps went into the fire and briefly smelled like potato chips as they dried out and burned up. Ted gathered a couple more armfuls of wood and then went to check on Zolly.

Out of sight on the south end of the pine grove, Zolly had used an army surplus entrenching tool to pry up a large flat stone and was in the process of carefully scooping out the sandy soil beneath. Stepping lightly, he carried each shovelful twenty feet to the shore and spread it out below the waterline. In ten or twelve trips, he had a round pit just a bit smaller than the footprint of the stone. He had found a rusted gallon can (there was a surprising amount of junk on the island) and fitted that into the hole. The coins filled about a quarter of the can. Ted and Zolly then gently tipped the stone back into place, and with their fingers combed a border of pine needles back around the edges. They were fussing at that when Buzzy came up holding a spoon and bringing the aroma of food on his clothes.

"Unda the stone?" he asked.

"Yah," the others chimed.

"Really good," he said, shaking his head. "Nobuddy's gonna find it there."

"'specially if nobuddy knows it's there," added Ted.

"It won't take long for somebuddy ta figure somethin' out if they find those busted slots," Zolly contributed.

"Let's hope we get 'em all before that happens," Ted replied.

They stood around contemplating that final thought and admiring their handiwork when a breeze carrying the smell of fish stew from the fire reached them.

Crouching on stones for seating, they watched as Buzzy put the final touch on his dish. Just before he served it, he mixed some powdered milk with water and added the mixture, fulfilling the requirement that transformed his soup into an official "chowda." The boys ate heartily for a while, joking about who was eating whose fish, but inevitably they came around to the events of the day. Though they couldn't be sure, the answer to how the boat got on the lake bottom likely had something to do with the wall at the mouth of the cove. The empty craft might have gone in and been loaded at the shore. With the extra weight, it could have caught the wall on the way out, and heavy as it was, it didn't get far. Hitting the bottom like an anchor, the boat had almost been swallowed by the thick mud. In another few years, when the ribs rusted away completely and the wooden boxes disintegrated, nobody would have ever known it was there. Almost certainly these events happened under the cover of night and were of course some sort of illegal activity. The boys then talked about the statute of limitations being seven years, but beyond that single fact they knew nothing about the legality of such matters. Once again, they arrived at the conclusion that the best strategy was recovering as much as they could before they told their tale. Besides, it was all just too much fun to let someone else do it.

Buzzy whipped up some biscuit dough, which they wadded onto green sticks and played over the coals until the dough baked up into something that resembled a large brown cocoon—crusty on the outside and a bit gummy on the inside.

The boys ate these delicacies after dipping them in grape jelly. By now it was getting dark, and in the ancient conspiratorial way of campfires, the friends drew closer for warmth and light. They flipped over Buzzy's cutting board and, in pencil, wrote down the number of fifty-cent and dollar coins, along with the total value of their haul and the date. They then passed the plank around, and each initialed it. The solemnity that they felt in carrying out this simple act surprised them. When Ted, who was last to sign, looked up at his friends, he knew that some new link had been forged between them—something a little deeper than had been there just minutes before. He could see they all felt that way, and he sat there in the orange light savoring the strange sensation.

Suddenly Zolly, with his usual abrupt manner, bolted up and began collecting the pots and pans. He and Ted went out by the boat, and with a little soap scoured the cookware clean in the sand. With an evening chill coming on, the lake water felt remarkably warm. As things were put away and the fire dwindled to a pile of gray embers, the campers noticed that mosquitoes had arrived in force. Rummaging around in the hammock, Ted came up with a heavy glass bottle of army-surplus insect repellent. The grimy label read "Citronella" and had a paragraph of instructions in tiny letters, something no fourteen-year-old would ever bother to read. They smeared on the syrupy yellow liquid, and it did repel insects. But the smell, which could be likened to lemons in only the most general way, was intense and relentless. With their necks and arms showing an oily sheen, they pulled on sweatshirts and headed for the Skunk's Nose.

The rounded boulder, about ten feet across and six feet high, was another product of glacial activity. Large as it was, it had been a mere pebble in the giant rivers of ice. Sometime in the thousands of years of the last ice age, a bit of rock had been broken off a formation way up north—Canada maybe—and had been tumbled and carried hundreds of miles to this spot. When the ice sheet retreated, this glacial erratic was neatly deposited on the surface. Stones like this were erratic in both their placement—scattered randomly in the landscape—and in the fact that they were not typical of the bedrock of southern New England. Skunk's Nose was not even a particularly large glacial erratic. This bit of geology was something they had learned in science class, but climbing up on it just then wasn't about science lessons. At least it was not about a formal science lesson. This was more applied science. The dark granite lump was situated just offshore, where, unshadowed in any way, it caught the full energy of the sun's rays. All day long it soaked up energy. By stretching out on its upturned face, the boys could tap into the warmth that was now radiated back out into space. The strategy also gave them a perfect view of the night sky, cloudless from horizon to horizon. With the moon not yet up, the Milky Way was on grand display across the infinitely deep blackness.

In the presence of such a sight, the excitement of their adventure slipped to second place. They couldn't stop themselves from discussing solar systems and galaxies and time. It was a constant wonder to them that the stars were really suns that might have planets circling them, and were so far away that the light they were seeing was already thousands of years old. From astronomy and science fact they drifted to another of their favorite topics: science fiction. Zolly retold a short story he had read about an advanced society that had completely vanished from its home planet but had built a huge clock that had dutifully continued to mark off the millions of years since they disappeared. Ted had read a story about an entire planet that was a single life form. At this point in their lives, they didn't so much discuss ideas as they tossed them out to marvel at. From science fiction, their talk devolved further to "Ripley's Believe It or Not," a syndicated newspaper feature that traded on the bizarre and the strange. Ted had seen one about a man who grew a four-inch horn out of the middle of his forehead. Zolly resisted believing anything he saw in "Ripley's," but in the darkness you could be persuaded to consider anything. They talked on about another man who, it was claimed, could see the stars in broad daylight. How could that be? Soon, however, the warmth of the stone and the exertion of the day began to have an effect. Conversation slowed and then stopped altogether as they drifted into drowsiness. When it dawned on them that they were falling asleep, they retired to the tent and their sleeping bags. No one brushed his teeth.

CHAPTER 5

Trail of Events

The sun was well up and the morning mist had burned off by the time Zolly crawled out of the tent, scratching and stretching. He was working his tongue around in his mouth to get some saliva going when Buzzy handed him a wedge of orange. "Mmmm" was all he could manage from behind the rind as he stuffed the whole thing into his mouth and sucked the juice. Ted had been up for a while and was coming back from washing. Buzzy, God bless him, had been up longest and was again crouched before the fire, where a skillet of bacon sizzled away. *There is nothing, nothing like the smell of bacon over a campfire,* Ted thought. Next to the bacon, Buzzy was boiling coffee. *The brown stuff again?* thought Ted, but he quickly resigned himself to the fact that it was everywhere and he might just as well learn to like it. Buzzy took three large potatoes out of the embers where he had nestled them the night before and scraped away a quarter inch of carbon to reveal nicely cooked centers. These he sliced into the bacon fat. Three eggs were being boiled in with the coffee water.

Ted reported that there was no one else on the pond, and that they would likely have the whole place to themselves for a second day. Zolly, expressing nothing so much as youthful enthusiasm, stripped off his underwear, grabbed his towel, gave a whoop, and sprinted off to plunge headlong into the lake. He came back, toweling himself vigorously, just as Buzzy was portioning out breakfast. Zolly put his folded towel on a rock and sat down naked to eat. After cleaning up and packing some lunch—peanut butter and jelly sandwiches and apples—they talked of their plans for the day. This time, they would bring their fishing poles as a pretense. It was an unwritten rule that you don't approach somebody who's fishing, so just having the rods out would be enough to keep anybody from getting close enough to see what they were really up to. They also brought the ax, a pair of leather work gloves that Buzzy used for cooking, and T-shirts and hats to keep off the broiling sun.

The day was clear and already hot. By this time in late August, the humidity of midsummer had diminished, and the chance of any serious rain was slim. In this part of the country, it was the driest time of year. The sky was as blue as New England had to offer. Puffy, fair-weather clouds drifted in a stately procession from west to east. Over the wreck, as they now referred to it, the boys propped up their fishing poles and began dropping and raising the anchors to smash up some of the boxes below. It took a few minutes for the bottom to settle down enough for Ted to make the first dive. With the gloves, he was able to probe around less cautiously than he had the day before. Their wrecking-ball strategy with the anchors had worked. As soon as he put his hand down, he could detect the rough decorative pattern on two machines that were leaning against each other. He felt around for one of the arms and cinched the rope around the first he came to. Before he could reach the surface, the others had taken up the slack, and as he hung onto the boat, he could look down to watch as the case came up, trailing the now familiar plume of mud. They hauled with such early-morning enthusiasm that the heavy machine looked something like a rocket blasting off and leaving a trail of smoke behind. Ted put his weight on the bow as the others lifted the first slot machine of the day up over the transom.

Again using the coiled rope as a kind of pad, they set to work—this time with a real tool. Using the back of the ax head as a sledgehammer, Buzzy was able to deliver several precise blows to the bottom edge of the case, where the rusted screws snapped one at a time. With fewer than eight hits, the insides spilled out, gushing water and debris that made it look like the machine had been gutted. Bits of brass and rusty iron sloshed about with the coins. Collecting and selling scrap metal—especially brass—was one of Ted's methods of earning spending money, and by force of habit he just couldn't bring himself to waste it. So two piles of metal grew, with one considerably more valuable than the other. Ted's fussing over the brass irked Zolly, as it slowed things down. The fact was, however, that with their excitement at such a high pitch, they would have exhausted themselves early on had they not somehow slowed their pace.

Any small bits of iron got thrown directly overboard, but so as not to confuse things later, they took the time to row off fifty feet or so before tossing in the cases and their insides. Working methodically from amidships to stern, they pulled up ten machines before Buzzy came upon the sunken boat's tiller. It was a simple galvanized pipe that had been attached to the head of the now-crumbled wooden rudder. He shoved it out of the way with hardly a thought.

There were no boxes beneath the sweep of the tiller, so they took a break for lunch. They rowed into the cove and tied up to a rock ledge that formed a natural wharf. As they ate their sandwiches in the shade of the trees, they speculated that this very shelf was more than likely the spot where the sunken boat would have been loaded. Ted could imagine a line of men moving crates from some idling trucks to the boat. The smugglers would have passed just a few feet in front of where the boys were now sitting. Even on a dark night, the activity would have been silhouetted against reflections off the water. Perhaps in this remote part of the lake, the smugglers didn't fear discovery and used the stark yellow glare of their headlights to illuminate the work area. The mellow burbling sound of the boat's exhaust would most certainly have been part of the scene.

"Wonder where they were goin'?" Ted mused out loud, knowing that his friends were probably both thinking the same thing. "Where's a road on the other side, Breezy Point? Were they takin' the stuff into town?"

"Trolley bed comes down close to the water just over the Connecticut line, before it cuts across the old Herrod's Farm," said Buzzy.

"So they loaded it on a train?" asked Zolly.

"I dunno," responded Buzzy. "They're crooks. They do things ya don't expect."

To avoid cramps in the water, they had an hour to kill after eating. The coins retrieved so far that day were counted and brought the total to about $400. That growing number, that dollars-and-cents value, loomed large in their minds, where it was having a profound effect. Each in his way began to swell with pride at their achievement. For the first time in their lives, the play of boys had transitioned into the work of men, and they reveled in the feeling. They were doing a job that had real meaning, and it was feeding a hunger they didn't know they had. Nervous prattle continued for a while and then tapered off as they drifted into contemplation while listening to the sounds of a late summer afternoon.

Ted noticed droning insects swirling around their heads. Birdcalls came from points high in the trees. The hollow plop of a jumping fish arrived at a low angle from across the cove. Water lapped the rocks. All of this existed inside a rustling sweep of August breeze that coaxed anything it could to move with a lazy hiss. Ted was thinking that this kind of listening was very adult, a mature kind of thing to do. A month ago, he felt, he had been a heedless child dashing from one thing to another throughout the day, picking up and then dropping activities with not a moment's reflection. Now, he thought, he would teach himself to savor the time between. He would string the events of his day together as a whole. In this particular moment, he would get as much as he could from just listening. His grandfather did it all the time. Indians in books always seemed to be practicing it, or pointing out to some cloddish white man that he should "listen." Hunters and fishermen improved their results with a liberal application of quiet. Ted was savoring the moment. The three of them were a team, they had a job that was going well, and the rewards were real. In fact, the moment was just about perfect, so he might have sat there longer if Zolly hadn't pointed out that the sun was advancing across the sky. "Time ta get back ta work," Zolly said, rallying them to the task.

From about one o'clock to three, they worked forward toward the engine compartment and pulled up four more machines. Between amidships and the bow, they came to a new group of crates. Smaller than the boxes that held the slot machines, these were made of a wood that was a bit more resistant to rot, so Ted had to go down with the ax and gloves to see what could be done. Choking up on the handle of the ax, he pushed the blade forward like a chisel and pried up a soggy lid. As he pushed the blade in farther, he both heard and felt the clink of metal on glass. With his gloved hand he reached in and touched what was obviously a bottle. It was, in fact, a whole case of bottles. In an instant, he knew what he had; in this context, there could be little doubt. He grabbed one and headed for the surface. For dramatic effect, he extended his arm, holding the bottle straight up over his head so that it broke the surface first. Even with his ears still below the water, he thought he could hear Buzzy and Zolly gasp.

None of them was really surprised to find liquor. After all, if there was gambling, could drinking be far away? Still, it was an exciting find. As Ted pulled himself into the boat, the others were already inspecting the new discovery. There was no label left—if the bottle ever had one—but its short neck and heavy glass betrayed it as the product of a Canadian distillery. Prohibition in the US had been a boon for the Canadians. Their own experiment with banning alcohol had failed, and perhaps they had a somewhat cynical attitude toward their American cousins. Among other things, they designed these stout short-necked bottles to hold up on the rough journey south that their product was likely to make. Again, Ted's uncle Steve had enlightened him on the subject and had even shown him an old bottle he kept around to support his story. This one was clear glass, so it was easy to see that the cork was still in fair shape, and the brown liquid that sloshed around beneath it looked unaffected by its stay on the lake bottom.

"Spoze it's whiskey?" asked Buzzy

"Most likely," answered Ted, who, because of his uncle, considered himself their expert on the subject. "But it could be anything: rum, or brandy, or bourbon, or gin even." His expertise didn't extend to knowing the obvious difference between whiskey and gin. "Looks like it's still good," he added with a touch of pomposity in his voice. The cork was darkened with decay for the first half inch of its length, but the remaining inch or so looked as good as new. They all sat down to ponder this development.

"Should we open it?" wondered Zolly.

"We're not spoze ta even have it," said Buzzy.

"Maybe there's somethin' wrong with it," Ted added.

They had all heard horror stories about poison whiskey from moonshiners, so they were not about to experiment.

"Anyway," said Ted, "if we were worried about them takin' the silver away from us, they sure as heck are gonna take this stuff."

They decided to look into a few more boxes and bring up a bottle or two as evidence. From the motor housing forward, they counted about forty boxes, each the size of the first one that had contained twelve bottles. There was not much else they could do. Their little rowboat couldn't hold all that liquor anyway, and even if they pulled it up, no one, as Ted had observed, would let them keep it. In fact, having that much whiskey associated with the coins might just make it more difficult to hold on to their treasure.

When Buzzy surfaced with a bottle filled with clear liquid, Ted's memory got jogged. "Oh, oh, yah, yah, vodka and gin are clear like water. That could be either of them," he said in a knowing tone intended to reestablish his authority on the subject.

"Heck," Zolly observed, "the staties"—that's what they called the state police—"are, fa sure, gonna get involved in this. It'll probably make the papers in Boston. There'll be lawyers and everathin'."

"Well, fa sure the whiskey is illegal, since it came over the Canadian border, but the coins are American money, it's not illegal ta have 'em," Ted mused. But again, they hit a wall. They had no idea what the law was on the matter.

"I know!" said Buzzy. "Let's only show some of the money and see what happens. We go home with fifty or seventy-five bucks and three bottles of this hooch. The state sends in divers. They bring up all the rest. They look at all the booze and say, aw, let the kids keep the few silver dollas."

"And if they take it all and say it belongs to the state of Massachusetts, what do we do then, give what we hid?" asked Zolly.

"Maybe," said Buzzy. "I dunno."

Ted restated the plan: "So we leave most of the money in the hiding place, and let everybody argue things out when the stakes aren't so high. If they say we get ta keep the fifty dollas, they'll have ta let us keep it all."

"It could work," said Buzzy, supporting the idea, "but we'd hafta keep it secret."

"Aw, secrets," moaned Ted as he slumped in his seat and drooped his head for a clowning effect. "I can't keep secrets."

"We kin do this! We kin do this!" said Buzzy, pressing his point enthusiastically.

They agreed. Other than showing up at home in a couple of days with three bottles of whiskey and a big bag of money, it was the only thing they could do to improve their chances of keeping anything. It didn't occur to them that they would have to lie when someone asked the obvious question, "Is this all you found?"

With some time on their hands, they made a few more dives on the wreck to look for, perhaps, a nameplate or even a bell. The prop, if it was still attached, would be buried in the mud deeper than they could reach. Besides, they had nothing to cut the shaft with if they did locate it. On what he thought was his last dive, Ted approached the site from a low angle across the bow, moving toward the stern as a cloud passed and the slanting rays of the four o'clock sun reached down to exaggerate the shadows. The area within the outline of the boat was plainly disturbed by their activity, but all around it the lake mud had maintained its smooth, velvety undulations. As he swam just a foot off the bottom, he noticed a series of subtle, evenly spaced bumps curving back a hundred feet toward the rock face at the front of the cove. They were low but stood out just enough against the monotonous bottom to form a curved line like a string of widely spaced beads.

Back in the boat, Ted posed the question, "What would you do if you was ta hit bottom and were leakin'? Maybe you knocked off the prop and were driftin'. What would be the first thing you would do?" Without waiting, he answered his own question: "Start throwin' stuff off, right?" He then described what he had seen.

"Da ya think that's what happened?" asked Buzzy.

"Looks like it ta me," said Ted.

They repositioned their boat over the first bump in the line, and Zolly went down. In no time (they were getting good at diving), he was back at the surface with a grin on his dripping face. "Looks like we got somethin' ta do tomorra," he said. "The one below us is definitely a slot, and I counted three more in the distance."

Amazing, thought Ted as they rowed back to camp. *This whole thing is a kind of story that's revealing itself in reverse.* Apart from the value of the silver and the significance of all that liquor, they were adding new information with each day, and a story was growing right out of the ground.

That night, it was a pound of fried bologna with peppers and onions and canned beans, with animal crackers for dessert. It was enough, but they would have eaten more if they had it. When they had cleaned up and counted the money—nearly five hundred dollars—they retired to the Skunk's Nose to catch the final glow of the sunset.

It had been a relatively easy day, and they had enough energy left to maintain their high spirits. As the stars came out, their conversation soared with boisterous enthusiasm, and they gleefully talked over one another. Words like *treasure* and *silver* and *fortune* and *whiskey* were sprinkled liberally among the fantasies of what each might do with his share. Not surprisingly, scuba gear was high on all three wish lists. Now that they were able to see the end of their labor, they allowed themselves to believe for the first time that the money could actually be theirs to keep. They suspended thinking in real-world terms and let their minds go. Looking up at the infinity of space, wishes were stated as facts and set free like bottle messages, tossed into the cosmos for some all-knowing power to read and fulfill. They floated on sheer youthful exuberance. Had the boys been a little more down-to-earth, it might have occurred to them to keep their voices low. The evening breeze was carrying their words to the nearby shore, where other, very human ears were listening.

><del></del>

Those ears belonged to Gus Ouellette, and he cared for nobody's wishes but his own. Small and rodent-like in both looks and character, he was the kind of parasite who hangs around more aggressive men for protection, snatching at little scraps as they came his way. He was a sneak who was always on the lookout for doors left unlocked or valuables left unattended. Even those who occasionally called him friend knew better than to trust him out of their sight. Gus had come down to the lake to check his setlines—an illegal type of fishing that used long anchored lines with many baited hooks. He kept an old square-nosed scow hidden in the bushes and tended the lines after dark. The previous night he had been in the same spot and noted the boys' presence, but either the wind was wrong or the boys were less energetic so he had heard nothing. Their presence on the island was dismissed as no more than a nuisance. Tonight, as the northerly breeze hastened sound over calm water, he was able to pick up the odd word—*money, whiskey.* When the air moved just right, he heard snatches of sentences with phrases like "my share" and "sunken treasure." He clearly heard someone say, "Lotta booze down there." And then he heard two words that set his mind to scheming: "More tomorrow." Gus knew the value of waiting and listening. He sat patiently in the bushes until he was sure the boys had gone to sleep, and then he tended to his business before skulking back into the woods with his dripping burlap sack of illegal fish—and something to think about.

CHAPTER 6

The Lady

Anyone who saw them anchored there for the third day would have assumed that this was, indeed, a good fishing spot. After all, what else was there to do in Mashpaug Lake?

The boxes that the boys now set their attention to had been thrown from the crippled boat and had hit bottom with force. They were not just dusted over by a carpet of fluffy silt; they had penetrated that relatively thin layer and were stuck in the dense black mud below. As a consequence, it took considerable work to open each and get the machines oriented for the rope. The first one was a hard pull and had no money in it. Thinking ahead, they had cut a long pole, with which they probed the mud from one bump to the next so as not to miss anything. Numbers two, three, and four were easier lifting and had money in them. The last one in the row brought them nearly to the rock face, only ten feet or so from where it rose up to support the stone wall. Poking around turned up two more completely buried machines. Perhaps the smugglers had gotten hung up on the rocks and started throwing them off to lighten the boat. The machines lay close together, and though the boys broadened their search to twenty feet in either direction, they found no more.

The afternoon was still young, so they decided to explore the rock face. Owing to the activity of the last few days, they had completely lost any fear of the murky underwater. In fact, as they surveyed it, the granite face began to look as familiar to them as any other outcropping on dry land. In some places, its top edge overhung the base by several feet; in others, the massive rock had shifted back, creating steps and narrow shelves. There were many long vertical cracks. Some of these opened less than a finger-width, while others were wide enough for the boys to swim into. Along its base were slabs of rock that had fallen and poked up through the mud. Climbing these walls on land was difficult sport and most often beyond any of their abilities, but here underwater, Ted felt like he was flying past them like a bird. He recalled pictures of coral walls from a *National Geographic* magazine at the dentist's office, though nothing so colorful as coral grew here.

Swimming ten yards to the right of where they had found the last slot machines, Buzzy explored an area where the top edge projected out and created an overhang. The dark undercut was deep enough for a swimmer to disappear into the shadow it cast. He descended hesitantly, feeling the rock face with one hand as he went. Near the bottom he began to make out a wide shelf almost even with the mud. It ran some fifteen feet from left to right, with a middle section as level and broad as a big desktop. Curiously, it had a long mounded area that occupied its center. Perhaps it was a sunken log. As he got closer, he could see that it was in fact a pile of loose rocks. He swept aside the thin layer of silt and pulled several stones down from about the middle of the mound. In the vacant spot, Buzzy saw something that struck him with terror. He recoiled in shock, kicking backward and pushing at the water with such force that the mask slid down around his neck. Blinded, he clawed his way to the surface, letting out bubbles of air in a silent scream as he flew upward. He broke the surface like a breaching whale, with half of his body out of the water before he crashed back in. Without a pause, he continued in a mad crawl to the boat and needed no help clearing the transom this time. Coughing and sputtering up the water he had swallowed in his panic, he was able to get out, "Bones. There's bones down there, I saw bones."

The others were now shocked as well. "What? Are you sure?" asked Ted.

"Yah, yah, I saw it: a bony hand."

For a moment, no one knew what to say. When Buzzy regained his composure, he gave them more details. Had someone drowned when the boat sank? It sounded more like a grave of some sort. What to do next? Zolly answered the unstated question by announcing, "I'm goin' down for a look." The others were grateful for his bold decision, and he had the gear on and was over the side before Ted could warn him to be careful.

It was like any of the other dives they had made in the last few days, but the shadowy recess and the possibility of bones gave even the reckless Zolly pause. He entered the dark shaft slowly, allowing time for his eyes to adjust to the low light as he went down. Sure enough, in the spot previously occupied by the stones, two or three stubby bones stained brown by the humus were visible. Zolly couldn't tell if they were really hand bones or not. In his young mind, he saw what lay before him as a test. What would a "man" do in a situation like this? Did he have the courage? Making a typically impulsive decision, he hardened his resolve and began to feel his way along through the silt toward the wider part of the mound, what he guessed must be the head. The carpet of silt was thinner here than on the adjacent bottom, and as he pushed rocks aside he glanced ribs and arm bones. Fortunately, there were no tatters of clothing or anything that looked like it might have once been flesh. At the top of the mound, he nudged off several rocks and was startled by what was obviously the smooth dome of a human skull, stained a uniform, lake-bottom brown. He pulled away more stones, and when he had exposed the skull enough, he reached under it and scooped the grizzly object into the clearer water. Inevitably, it trailed billows of lake dust. The vacant eye sockets and nose were plugged with mud. With his air running out, Zolly characteristically decided to go for the dramatic. Imitating Ted's theatrical entrance with the bottle, he swam to the surface holding his ghoulish prize straight up at arm's length over his head.

On the surface, the day was still. The breeze had dropped, and the lake had barely a ripple. What Ted and Buzzy saw as they stared at the water was a bit of staging that took full advantage of one of life's more shocking props. As the skull began breaking the surface, its tan roundness first appeared like some strange oversized egg. Zolly slowed his ascent. The forehead and then the ghastly eye sockets came into view. The vacant nasal opening came up, and finally the gap-toothed upper jaw pressing into Zolly's palm completed the tableau. As the skull rose higher, mud and water from the brain case drooled out, and black rivulets ran over Zolly's fingers and down his forearm. It might as well have been blood. Ugly sludge oozed from the nose, eyes, and ear holes. As he swam to the stern holding his prize aloft, the others backed toward the bow. When he dropped the skull roughly onto the rear seat, several teeth appeared to skitter loose.

Sensing that he might have gone too far, Zolly chided the others as he pulled himself up: "Aw, come on, it's only some old bones." He picked the cranium up casually and sloshed it in the lake to rinse off the remaining mud. In truth, it looked better for his effort, more like a laboratory specimen. The skull now appeared surprisingly small in Zolly's hands, and its sloping eye sockets seemed more sad than threatening. When they inspected the muddy nuggets that had rattled on the seat, the boys found that they were not teeth at all but beads—small tubes of a dull white material. There were three, all the same size, just under a quarter inch around and little over a half inch long. The boys recognized them as something they had seen in a display case at the Historical Society. Such shell beads, called wampum, were a common trade item among the coastal Indians before the white man arrived. Once again, the story had expanded right in front of them. Had they stumbled onto an ancient gravesite? How old was it? Were there more bodies down there?

And again, there was only one way to find out. Over the next hour, they made a general survey of the entire rock face and didn't come up with any other shelves wide enough to lay a body on. The section under the overhang was the only place, and it had room for just one. Perhaps because the skull was small or because there were beads, the boys all began to think of it as "she." Ted and Buzzy were emphatic on one point: "She" had to go back in place before they left. "Aw, okay, I'll put her back," Zolly grudgingly agreed, "but let's keep the beads."

It was agreed. Zolly went down once more to lay the head back in place, and as he nestled it in the mud, even he felt this was the right thing to do. He couldn't, however, stifle his curiosity, and after using their probing stick to estimate the length of the skeleton (about five feet), he let his hands wander into the area that would have been the skeleton's neck and chest. Sure enough, there were many more beads. As he grabbed for a handful, his gloved fingers closed on something flat and long. When he drew his fist out, he could see that he was holding a stone knife. It was an elegantly made tool, translucent white with a handle that was notched at the pommel, perhaps for tying to a lanyard. The blade was about five inches long and had the familiar pressure-flaked edge of most stone tools. In another impulsive instant, he decided that he would keep it and hide his discovery from the others. Carefully, for it was still sharp, he rolled the blade into the back waistband of his swim trunks. Back in the boat, he quickly put on his T-shirt to conceal his secret. On their row back to the island, they all agreed that returning the skull was the right thing to do, but that taking a few beads wasn't exactly grave-robbing.

"Besides, what would we do with a skull?" Ted asked. Then, elaborating on his thought of the previous day, "What would happen if we showed up at home with a bag of money, three bottles of whiskey, and a human skull?"

"Ya mutha would faint," Buzzy retorted, and the two laughed heartily.

Zolly was silent.

Rowing back to the island, they discussed the day. On the point of how such a grave got down that deep, they knew that it must have been underwater even before Samuel Slater built his dam, but only by ten or so feet. Had someone deliberately put it underwater, or had the lake been even lower in the far-distant past?

It had been a long day, and it was well after sunset before the boys finished supper. They were counting the day's find and had just added it to their tally board when they heard voices from the beach. Hurriedly they hid the evidence, but hadn't gotten far when two men with a hurricane lantern rounded the bushes into the firelight. One was Gus Ouellette. The other was Dickey Herrod. The boys knew both men by reputation. Dickey announced himself with, "Howdy, boys. So, how da ya like my little island here?"

Chapter 7

Herrod's Swamp

Cassimere Herrodofski had come from Poland to Slaterville in 1907 to work in the mills—not to mention avoid the draft for the Prussian Army. America's growing industries needed labor, and an agent for the Logan Fabric Company paid for his passage from Hamburg to New York. Someone on this side of the Atlantic had whisked him and a few others through Ellis Island so fast he could never be sure he had even seen the place. He was on the factory floor, working, the same day he unpacked his meager belongings in a small room at a company boardinghouse in Slaterville. Severe and irascible, he was also hardworking. After four friendless years of double shifts, he had saved enough to put a down payment on an abandoned farm located over the state line at the south end of Mashpaug Lake. In another year, he had the money to bring a bride over from Poland.

The land was cheap because, after Slater's inundation, a good deal of what had once been fields and pastures now existed as ponds and marshes. The state of Connecticut claimed some jurisdiction over wetlands, so the old deeds and their boundary lines were confused. Land from one piece of pre-deluge property was cut off from the original parcel and was reachable now only by boat or by traveling ten miles around in order to cross someone else's land for access. No one had bothered to sort it all out. There was, however, enough good land recorded on Herrod's deed (Cassimere Herrodofski had changed his name to Carl Herrod) for a single man and his wife to eke out a living growing vegetables and chickens and selling eggs. Once a week, in season, Carl would load up the wagon and take his products to town. His wife, Theta, having come directly from the Old Country, never learned English and never left the farm. She was virtually a prisoner to the place. Few people actually saw her.

On his return from town, Carl was usually drunk and violent. Theta often had to run off to the woods to avoid a beating, later sneaking back to sleep in the barn until Carl had sobered up. After a couple of years, they stumbled onto good fortune when the trolley line was extended south and the railroad paid Carl for the right of way. With the extra money, life became less desperate, and Dickey, their only child, was born in 1918. Things remained calm until 1920, when the United States enacted Prohibition, banning the manufacture, transportation, import, export, and sale of alcohol and alcoholic beverages. Always enterprising and contemptuous of Americans' idealistic attitude toward alcohol, Carl quickly fashioned his own still and became one of the first moonshiners in the area, selling pints he hid under the radishes and beets. Most people knew what was going on but encouraged Carl's business with "a wink and a nod." Almost all of his customers were European immigrants who, like himself, saw the banning of alcohol as the overly optimistic experiment of a young country.

Life on the farm changed dramatically in the midtwenties when two gentlemen from Providence, Rhode Island, approached Carl with a "business" proposition. The men were career criminals scouting routes for moving liquor south from Canada. By that time, smuggling "Canadian hooch" had developed into a serious contest between organized crime and the police. Immense amounts of money were at stake; it was no longer a matter of selling a few pints of moonshine off the back of a wagon. These men knew Carl's situation, and though he eagerly agreed to work for them, they would have had no problem using his illegal activity as leverage. What they needed was his location, his wagon, and his barn. His job was to keep up his little side business as a front; they would bribe any local officials if necessary. Then, under the cover of night, Carl could regularly rendezvous with a boat at the spot where the railroad bed ran along the lake shore. No trains moved along the sleepy little line at night, so he could easily make two or three trips back and forth to the barn. He met the boat once, sometimes twice a week, and every two weeks a truck with lettering that proclaimed "Providence Fruit Company" would make a pickup. The money was excellent—so good, in fact, that Carl was able to build a fine new house and bring in electricity and a telephone line.

At times, it seemed too good to be true. There were dozens of ways they could have been discovered, but the system worked. No one ever found out. The problem was the Twenty-First Amendment, which repealed Prohibition in 1933. Overnight, the money stopped. Coincidentally, the trolley company went out of business. With his savings, Carl tried to expand his farming operation. He bought some additional acreage and hired seasonal help, but in the end, he was no manager. He tried to make up the difference by doubling his own effort, but that was a desperate strategy and doomed to fail. As his income became smaller, his anger grew, and he took out his frustration on his wife and growing son. He drank more and got into arguments with his customers in town. The situation was in a downward spiral. When Dickey was old enough, he moved out.

One day, Carl showed up at the police station to report that his wife had gone out berry-picking two days earlier and had never come back. Search parties were organized, but nothing was ever found. It was Dickey who noticed that his mother's berrying pail was still hanging in the barn. He accused his father of the worst, but the police could do nothing. There was no evidence. After that, Dickey left town, disappearing for years. Some said he wound up in jail. Carl turned more deeply in on himself and actively drove people away. He farmed enough to feed himself and rarely went into town. The buildings slipped into disrepair. Paint peeled and the clapboards curled. The electricity and phone were cut off. In a few years, the house and barn looked almost abandoned. Weeds grew up through the porch floor and an unattended leak in the barn roof set a whole loft full of hay to rotting. During a cold snap one late winter, someone passing on the nearby road noticed that there had been no smoke from the chimney for several days. Police went into the icy house and found Carl dead, frozen to a chair. An autopsy revealed that he had died of undiagnosed liver cancer. It must have been a tough way to go.

That spring, Dickey drifted back to town and took up residence in the old place. His life away must have been hard, for he returned a violent and brooding man himself.

Almost immediately, he got into trouble with the law, mostly from drinking and fighting. In his time away he had somehow acquired skills as an auto mechanic, but he never worked anyplace for long. Most jobs ended with arguments or accusations of petty theft. For a while he attracted a few characters like himself, and the house became a hangout for the unsavory element of the town. It was briefly famous as a place for drinking and rowdy card games. That's how Dickey came to know Gus.

Gus insinuated himself into Dickey's life by simply drinking himself unconscious night after night and waking up on the floor in the mornings. He began to contribute to the household—drinks mostly—and he cooked. By yielding to Dickey in almost everything, he carved out a niche for himself. Between the two of them, they managed to hold on to the place, which is to say they made irregular payments to the tax collector and not much else. They heated with wood in the winter and suffered all summer with the mosquitoes and flies that came in through the broken windows. As rooms became unlivable, they boarded them off, retreating to smaller and smaller spaces.

From the day Theta's disappearance became known, the common belief was that Carl had killed her and that her body was buried somewhere on the property—or more likely sunken, piled with stones, in the swamp. People naturally avoided the place. The continued decline of its buildings only contributed to its eeriness.

In one sense, Dickey and Gus used the little bit of power that people's fear brought, but at the same time they nursed a mutual grudge against the world. They supported each other in the opinion that everything was just their bad luck, and that life had dealt them both a bad hand. They agreed that they were justified in doing whatever they had to, to get along.

Those attitudes led them into many conflicts. Mr. Morracy had once caught Gus snooping around the marina at night and put in outdoor lighting because of the incident. He recently suspected that it was Gus who had taken a bundle of dirty uniforms that had been left outside the door for the cleaning service to pick up. Then Mr. Samulski had an encounter with Dickey when he arrived unusually early at the bakery one morning and found Dickey testing a back window with a pry bar. Voices were raised, and Dickey threatened Stan Samulski. To protect himself, Ted's father had filed a police report, and the investigation had further enraged Dickey. Many people in town had similar stories.

Dickey Herrod was perhaps the only living person who knew about the sunken boat off Frenchman's Cove. His father had never taken him into his confidence regarding the nighttime activities; Carl didn't talk much. However, the young Dickey was alert enough to notice that there was a disruption in the traffic of boxes through the barn. He gleaned enough from conversations to know that a significant event, having to do with a boat sinking, had happened. All these years he had suspected that there was whiskey sitting on the bottom of the lake, but he had no way to get at it himself. When Gus came back with an account of the boys' conversation, things fell into place, and Dickey had smiled, thinking that providence had put an opportunity right into his hands. Unfortunately, when he and Gus climbed into the scow to paddle out to Skunk Island, they had no plan in mind. They never planned anything, and that lack of foresight set the stage for events to go very wrong.

Chapter 8

Abduction

As the two men stood there in the dim light, the most obvious thing about them was how much larger Dickey was than the scrawny Gus. What Ted noticed next was that both men had on dark blue uniform pants that looked to be the same size but fit neither of them. On Gus, they were far too big, and he had them cinched up with a length of rope that served as a belt. On Dickey, the top button was strained to the point of failure under the weight of his belly, and the cuffs were an inch short of his ankles. His shirt, which fit him, was a tan uniform type, with "Dickey" embroidered over one pocket and "Slaterville Shell" over the other, an obvious leftover from one of his short periods of employment. Both men were shiny with sweat, and both had a day's growth of whiskers. Dickey's black hair was plastered in tiny wet curls along his temples, and he was still red in the face from the exertion of rowing. Gus, who was mostly bald, had deep-set eyes and waxy yellow skin that reminded the boys of a certain skull they had seen recently. His scrawny neck and bony shoulders enhanced the skeleton effect, as did the fact that he stood a step behind Dickey, deeper in the shadows.

Ted had flipped over the tally board to cover the coins, and Zolly hid the bottles behind his back. As Dickey advanced, there was nothing more to see than three boys sitting at a campfire.

He rephrased his first statement. "Ya know this is my property."

Ted doubted that.

"Who are you boys?" the big man demanded.

They gave their first names.

"No, I mean ya last names," he insisted. That's the way things worked in a small town: you were known by your family connection before you were known as an individual.

When Ted said Samulski, Dickey halted him. "Stan Samulski your father?"

"Yes," answered Ted.

"Your old man's a jerk," growled Dickey.

Oh my god, this is not going well, Ted thought to himself. *Don't do anything stupid, keep your mouth shut.* He stifled his impulse to defend his father and felt diminished for it.

At this point, Gus caught a glint off one of the bottles and scuttled over behind Zolly. "Well, my oh my, what do we have here?" he cackled as he brought one into the light.

"Gimme that," said Dickey.

Gus obediently delivered it into his hands.

Dickey studied the bottle in silence for a moment. "Where'd ya get this?"

The boys looked down at the tally board. *How much does this guy know?* they were all thinking. *What should we say?* In a community where children were taught to respect adults, there was no option. They were good boys, and on the spur of the moment they could think of no reasonable lie.

"Over by Frenchman's Cove," replied Zolly.

Without hesitation Dickey followed with, "Is there more of it?"

"Some," said Zolly.

"How much?" persisted Dickey. "A lot?"

Buzzy jumped in with, "We don't know."

"More though, huh?"

"Yah," mumbled someone.

"Well, it's mine," said Dickey. "Whatever's down there is all mine."

Nobody said anything was down anywhere, thought Ted. *This guy knows something.*

Dickey went on, "It was my father's, and now it's mine. Tell ya what," he added, "you guys can pay me back for trespassing on my island by gettin' what's there for me tomorra."

"Yah," the three agreed in unison, their eyes unintentionally fixed on the tally board as if it were transparent. Agreeing to his demand might get rid of this guy. Ted jumped up and fetched the two other bottles as a show of good faith.

Actual distilled liquor was a rare prize for the two men, and waving the bottles in front of Gus's face caused him to swing his head from side to side as if he were watching a hypnotist's pendulum.

"Lots better'n squeezins," Gus mumbled.

For the past few weeks, Dickey and Gus had been drinking Sterno. "Squeezins," as they called it, was made by straining a cooking fuel, also known as canned heat, through cloth to separate the alcohol from a blue jelly that made it safe to handle. The resulting liquid didn't taste like much, but it was cheap and potent, one of the last resources of a down-and-out alcoholic. It was also subtly poisonous. Gus couldn't contain his anticipation as he rubbed his hands together and glanced back and forth from Dickey's face to the bottle he held.

"Maybe we should check it out ta make sure it's still good," he said.

"It's good," Dickey said in a vague tone that indicated wheels were turning in his head. He, too, was entranced with the sight of a real drink just the other side of a cork. Clearly neither man would go another step without sampling what they now considered their property.

Gus produced a folding knife and went to work on one of the other bottles. With the small blade, he poked away at the cork, breaking off bits, until there was about a half inch of it left. Then he picked up a stick and pushed that little nub down. This maneuver produced a squirt of amber liquid that shot up and hit Gus in the face. He laughed as he licked a drip from the corner of his mouth.

"Tastes fine," he grinned. "Rum, I think."

"Take a real drink," commanded Dickey.

Gus understood what he was being asked to do. He shifted nervously from one foot to the other, and then he wiped his mouth with the back of his hand and raised the bottle to his lips. His Adam's apple bobbed once. He lowered the bottle and waited with an expectant look on his face. Thirty seconds, a minute … nothing happened. Dickey could control himself no longer; he snatched the bottle from Gus and took a pull.

"It's rum all right," he said decisively.

He handed the bottle back to Gus, who was already eager for another swallow. Then Dickey inspected the other bottles. "Gin or vodka," he pronounced over one. "Looks darker than the first," he said of the other.

An open bottle in the hands of these two drunks was an irresistible temptation. They each took a few more swallows.

"Wanna drink?" teased Dickey. He extended the open bottle toward the boys. Then, as if he'd made a joke, he snatched it back with a "Hah!"

Seeing an opportunity to move things in another direction, Ted jumped in with, "So, tomorra we'll bring more of it up for ya?"

Dickey's concentration had wandered as the alcohol began to circulate in his system, but even so, it dawned on him that tomorrow was a long way off. It didn't take much imagination to suppose that if he left the island for the night, the boys would be gone by morning, and with them his chance of getting his hands on more of this stuff.

"Tell ya what," he drawled, stroking his double chins, "no sense you fellas sleepin' on this buggy old island. You can stay at my place tonight, then we can all go together in the mornin'."

"Nah, that's all right," protested Ted.

"No, I want ya ta come," Dickey said in a tone of false politeness that made it clear he was not extending a casual invitation.

"We'll be all right," Ted insisted.

"Nah, ya betta come with us," Dickey countered. "Ya might get eaten by mosquitoes or somethin'. Get ya stuff and come on."

At this point, Dickey's left foot was just inches from the tally board. The boys hoped that by moving to the tent, they could draw him in that direction, away from the fire. With a fair amount of commotion, they gathered up their sleeping bags. Gus followed and stuck his nose in the tent, where he fished out Ted's flashlight.

"Hey, we kin use this." He cackled as he switched the flashlight on and off several times like a new toy.

Who's we? Ted wondered.

Dickey hadn't moved an inch; he had simply turned his head to watch the proceedings. He reeled a bit. With the second tide of alcohol rushing into his brain, he was a little unsteady on his feet, so when he actually moved to go he staggered a bit, stepping back to correct his balance. His heel came down on the tally board and levered it up on one end. As he regained his balance and stepped off, the board came back down on the pile of coins. The sound was distinct—the sharp ring of silver money. Everyone froze. Though tipsy, Dickey was not yet stupid drunk.

"What the ..." he grumbled as he kicked the board out of the way. His eyes fixed on the small pile of silver dollars. Gus darted over and the two began to grab up the money. Dickey turned to the boys with a fistful of coins and pine needles. "What's dis?" he demanded. "You didn't say nuthin' about no money."

That question left the boys with only one possible response. Zolly made it: "Ya didn't ask."

At this point, Gus jumped in. "See, I told ya I heard 'em say sumpthin' 'bout treasure."

"Where'd ya get it, Mr. Smart Aleck?" Dickey growled.

"From the sunken boat," said Buzzy. Glancing over at the tally board, which had fortunately landed with the writing side down, he added, "There was some slot machines; that was in 'em."

It was news to Dickey that there had been slot machines in with the shipments of booze. "Are there more?" he questioned.

"We don't think so," Ted answered.

"Well, we're gonna look special good tomorra and make sure there ain't no more. Cuz whatever is down there belongs ta me. Let's get goin'," said Dickey, jerking his thumb toward the boats.

>∿∿

On the beach, Dickey made Gus turn over all the coins he had. He then patted the man's pockets to make sure Gus wasn't holding anything back. He carried out this procedure in grim silence as Gus meekly tolerated the indignity.

"I'll row them," said Dickey. "You bring the scow."

There was no real beach on the opposite shore. Gus's low scow could sneak in under the overhanging bushes, but the boy's high, slab-sided rowboat had to plow a path through the branches before it hit shore. Climbing onto dry land was a scratchy business, especially while carrying sleeping bags. When they assembled under the trees just behind the bushes, it would have been pitch black if not for the soft orange flame of Dickey's lantern. When Gus got his boat secured, he switched on the flashlight, but it was still a new discovery to him and he blinded everybody by flashing it in their faces.

"Put that damn thing out," growled Dickey, squinting and waving off the bright electric beam.

As Gus fumbled with the flashlight, one of the two bottles he had been cradling in his arms slipped out and smashed on the rocky ground. In an instant, Dickey roared as if he'd been physically hurt and sprang toward Gus with a look of pure malice in his tiny eyes.

"Take it easy, take it easy," Gus pleaded as he stepped back, waving his palms frantically, "there's plenny more where that come from, you'll see, you'll see. Tomorra there'll be lots, you'll see, we won't be able ta drink it all."

Halted as much by the chance of stepping on broken glass as by Gus's argument, Dickey abruptly stopped his charge and settled down almost as quickly as he had exploded. The suddenness and violence of the outburst—and its equally sudden disappearance—terrified the boys. It was weird, not like any human reaction they had ever experienced. Ted found himself trembling.

"Let's go, and don't drop that other bottle," warned Dickey.

There was a path that led directly away from the shore. Dickey went first, followed by the boys, and Gus brought up the rear. Under the trees the brush was thinner, but their single-file line still had to spread out at about six-foot intervals so that no branches snapped back into the next person's face. The boys' bulky sleeping bags seemed to get hooked on every twig anyway. The footing was tricky too, so they all watched Dickey's light and noted any obstacles as he stepped around them. They hadn't gone a hundred yards when the path opened up and joined another that ran east to west. Dickey then decided that it was the time and place for another drink. He set the lantern down, took his thumb off the open bottle he had been carrying, and raised the liquor to his lips. Then Gus took his turn.

God, thought Ted, *if they keep this up, they won't make it to the farm.*

"Okay, let's go," said Dickey, nodding toward the east.

At the word *go,* Zolly took off on a dead run in the opposite direction. All the boys knew approximately where they were, and any of them could have found his way home, even in the dark. Zolly was running away. He got about fifty feet before Gus, fumbling with the flashlight, caught him in its beam. What happened next was difficult to say. Had the light startled him, or had he looked over his shoulder to see what was happening? Whichever it was, Zolly stumbled and went sprawling into the duff of the forest floor, nearly knocking himself unconscious. Fortunately, he didn't hit any rocks. In an instant Gus was at him, his bony hand jerking him to his feet. Zolly stumbled back to the group with the little man goading him from behind.

"So this is how you treat my hospitality," Dickey said without a hint of irony in his voice. "We can't have this, now can we?"

As Zolly labored to regain his breath and Buzzy reached out to comfort him, Gus announced, "I got a idea. Wait here, I'll be right back." He scurried down the path toward the boats and returned in a few minutes with a length of rope cut from an anchor line. He then proceeded to tie one end, loosely, around Zolly's neck. Then he let out a few feet and tied another loop around Buzzy's. The tail end of the rope went around Ted's neck. With his belly full of rum, Gus seemed to take pleasure in his handiwork and was even humming to himself as he tied the knots.

This is a bad situation getting worse, Ted thought. *Best to keep the mind focused; this thing is getting seriouser and seriouser.*

"Let's go, and no funny business this time," warned the big man. Tied together and forced to stumble through the woods in the dark, all the boys realized, for the first time, that a clearly criminal act was being committed. A bullying invitation to spend the night was one thing. A rope around the neck felt a lot like kidnapping. Ted wondered if that thought had occurred to Dickey, and another layer of dread flooded over him.

The east-running path was easier walking, and the boys could reach up and hold the knot around their necks to absorb any jerking in the rope, but it still managed to throw their balance off. After a quarter mile, the path turned southwest. Ted made mental notes of their route. He assumed that Buzzy, at least, was doing the same. That foot trail weaved for most of a half mile and went over a few stone walls, but as far as Ted could tell it didn't fork or meet any other path. Then, all of a sudden, they popped out onto the old trolley line. The iron rails had been torn up years ago, but the wooden ties were left behind. Even in the darkness they could see a third of a mile north to where the trees thinned out and the arrow-straight railbed lay in tangent to the curving lakeshore.

Dickey and Gus paused long enough for another drink and to catch their breath. Both men were puffing. They then headed south where the line of rotting sun-bleached ties marched into a dark tunnel of overhanging trees. Desperately, Ted tried to fix some landmark that would locate the junction with the path from which they had emerged, but train tracks are defined by their regularity, and in the faint light, he could find nothing distinctive. In another quarter mile, they came to a stone wall that paralleled the tracks on their right. The wall was one border of the Herrod property. In another fifty yards they reached a rickety barway. Several horizontal poles were fit into a crude ladder structure on either side of a cart road that headed west, toward the farmhouse. Nearly grown over now, the disused path was the very route Carl Herrod had taken for those many trips between the lake and his barn. Getting through the bars while roped together was an awkward business. Because of his great girth, it was a tight squeeze for Dickey. When they regrouped on the other side, they followed the cart road past fields that hadn't been tilled in years. Dickey did no farming, and slowly nature was reclaiming the ground that generations of farmers had labored so hard to clear from the forest. Sumac, blueberry, and poison ivy were the first rank of the invasion, advancing inward from the edges of the abandoned plots. In a few years, poplars would find an opportunity to spring up in dense, flagpole-straight thickets. Eventually, native hardwoods would overshadow those trees and grow to maturity, completing the reclamation process. The stone walls would be the only evidence that this had once been farmland. A line of trees shadowed the cart road until it came to a vast open field beyond which, directly opposite, they could see the house and barn of Herrod's place. The two main buildings stood out on a small rise surrounded by still-open fields. At a distance, they both looked quite solid. In the pale starlight, their silvery-gray siding reminded Ted of marble and Greek temples.

The barn was typical of the region, wood with a gambrel roof that covered a second-story hayloft. Its front doors rested on level ground and faced the house, but as the terrain sloped down to the back, a wedge of stone foundation was evident for about two-thirds of the barn's length. The last third of the structure was an overhang supported at the corners by massive wood posts. It was a common design that took advantage of the hilly ground and allowed a farmer to pull equipment in out of the weather, or to drop loads of manure down through a trapdoor in the floor above. Fifty feet away, opposite the barn, the house faced south. Beyond the two buildings to the west, the surrounding fields dipped at first and then rose up across a few acres of steep pastureland to a wooded ridge, beyond which ran Windham Road, State Road 173. Access to the farm was down a winding dirt road that descended from the highway. The house, eight rooms divided between two stories, was in a classic Greek revival style with molded square columns at the four corners and a complete triangle pediment, front and back, under the low saddle roof. A wide columned porch ran across the front and along the west side, back to the kitchen. All the windows were large. Four sets of French doors gave access from the porch to the ground-floor front rooms. Glass panels framed the entrance door.

As they moved closer, the two structures began to reveal their years of neglect. The house's lack of paint had left its siding so cupped and weathered that many boards had pulled off their nails and fallen to the ground. The porch on the west side had lost most of its roof, and the beautiful columns were collapsing in rot. Vines had grown up the backside of the house and into several broken windows. As they arrived at the front steps, Ted could see that the whole front was sagging into a subtle frown, a sure sign of serious decay. And as he looked over at the barn, he saw that it was leaning a few degrees to the east. Both buildings were probably beyond repair.

CHAPTER 9

Cadman Oliver

"Go on," said Gus, pushing Ted forward.

It was a step up to the porch. The weathered boards groaned under the weight of all five of them. Dickey had to bump the sagging door with his hip to get it open, and it scraped the floor as it swung away against the wall. The entry hall was musty. The wallpaper was stained and curling away at the top. Directly in front of them, the stairs to the second floor were thick with dust and had no footmarks on the treads—they hadn't been used in some time. The doors to the back rooms were boarded over with rough planks. Empty bottles and other junk were scattered everywhere. Dickey turned into the room on his right, which Ted thought must be the living room. There was no good furniture to be seen; that had been sold off long ago. The large space was now the men's primary living quarters, with two iron cots against opposite walls toward the front, a woodburning cookstove at about the midpoint along the east wall, and at the back a kitchen sink propped awkwardly near the corner. Its waste line had no trap and seemed to go straight out through the exterior wall. Scattered almost randomly were various wood and cardboard boxes, many rickety-looking chairs, and at least three cluttered tables. The fireplace on the west wall was also boarded over. A decorative plaster rosette in the middle of the ceiling, vestige of better days, no longer had its electric fixture, and someone had pulled out a few feet of the dead wiring as a hook to hang a kerosene lantern. As Dickey reached over to light the suspended lantern, he caught Ted eyeing two cases of Sterno piled near the door.

"Fell off a truck," he said. That meant they had been stolen somehow.

"Won't need those fa drinkin' no more," remarked Gus.

Dickey, indicating the cot against the outside wall, said, "Siddown, makes ya selves comftable."

Still tied together, the boys shuffled through the clutter and, with some adjustments to the rasping rope, sat on the sagging mattress. For the first time, they were able to look at each other and share their fear. The bed was anything but comfortable. It drooped toward the middle, forcing them together, elbow to elbow, like the three proverbial monkeys. Too intimidated to speak, they watched as Dickey cleared space on the table under the hanging light, where he set the bottles and the lantern that he was carrying. Gus lit another lantern that had a sooty chimney and put it on the mantle. With three flames going, the center of the room was reasonably bright.

From the sink, Gus retrieved two smudged glasses, and chairs were dragged into place at the table facing the boys. Dickey and Gus were settling in for some serious drinking. There was still over a bottle and a third of liquor left. Ted wondered if it would be enough. From experience, he knew that men like these two would probably try to drink it all. The only thing the boys could hope for now was that their captors would drink themselves into a stupor and fall asleep. Mill towns were hard-drinking places, and Slaterville was no exception. The boys had all seen their share of public and private drunkenness. Ted considered what kind of drunk Dickey would be when he got really loaded. Some became "happy" drunks; Gus showed signs of being one of those. Dickey, on the other hand, was more than likely the mean type—but you couldn't always tell.

With a couple more swallows in him, Dickey began to question the boys. How did they find the boat? Where, exactly, was it? How many more cases of bottles were there? Were they sure there were no more slot machines? All those questions could be answered with varying shades of truth and little risk—but not all questions are equal or intended to be so. When Dickey asked if they had told anyone else about their find, Ted's blood ran cold. Significant events could depend upon how he responded. He opted for vagueness: "Well, I did mention I saw somethin' to Mr. Morracy and Ed Town," he offered.

Before Dickey could respond, Buzzy jumped in with, "People know we're here, they'll be lookin' for us."

With a scowl of contempt, Dickey responded, in a cold threatening voice, "Things happen down this end of the lake that nobody knows about. You heard about my ma? She just disappeared, ya know."

"Wait a minute, wait a minute," said Ted, "we said we're gonna help ya." As he was saying this, he had the opportunity to look deeply into Dickey's face for the first time. The man's eyes were glassy, vacant. Whether it was the poison of the alcohol or the poison of his life, Dickey Herrod's mind seemed somewhere else. His brain was at least partly occupied with things not apparent to anyone else in the room.

Suddenly, there were footsteps on the porch. Hoping that

somehow the police had arrived, Ted's heart began to beat wildly. The drumming in his chest leapt into his throat when he heard the front door open. In a second, the outline of a man appeared highlighted by the orange light against the darkness of the hallway. The figure was short and had on a dark suit jacket, indistinct pants, and beat-up old dress shoes with no socks or laces. Ted could clearly see the bare skin of his ankles. On his head was a faded gray fedora. The face was dark, almost invisible in the shadow of the hat's wide brim. Ted's hope evaporated when Dickey glanced over his shoulder and said in a familiar tone, "Cadman, ya son of a bitch, c'mon in, mighta known you'd show up soon as we gut somethin' decent ta drink." In truth, it was not unusual for this man to drop by at odd hours. As he stepped further into the light, Ted immediately recognized him as another one of the town's outsiders, someone who often walked the woods alone at night.

Cadman Oliver was in his late fifties. A long gray braid hung forward over one shoulder, and the hat had a turkey quill tucked into its band. His skin was dark, almost the color of a penny, and deeply rutted from a life lived out-of-doors in all weather. His cheekbones were broad and so high they seemed to force his dark eyes into a permanent squint. It was said that he was the last full-blooded Nipmuck, the native tribe that had occupied the area long before Columbus or the Pilgrims. He was also someone who existed on the fringes of the community, but Mr. Oliver, as he was known, had none of the reputation of Dickey or Gus. For most of his life, he had eked out a living selling what could be gathered from forest and field. In each season, he could be found on Main Street with handwoven baskets and whatever he was able to collect. In summer, he had mushrooms and buckets of berries; in the fall, nuts. He often had bunches of whatever wildflowers were in bloom. The local game warden generously neglected his responsibility and looked the other way when Cadman showed up with a couple of pheasants out of season. Some people even ordered wild rabbits that he delivered fresh to their kitchen doors. In mid-December, he was a source for princess pine and laurel for Christmas wreathes. He also did odd jobs, like splitting and stacking wood. He did some yard work.

With his meager earnings, Cadman liked to go to the movies. Ted had often seen him coming out of the local theater at the end of the Saturday matinee; he apparently enjoyed watching the double features with the kids. For years, Cadman Oliver had lived with his sister in a small run-down apartment, but when she died he walked away from the place and built himself a tarpaper shack on some neglected land out near the Harriman State Forest, just over the line in Connecticut. He explained himself by saying, "She was the only person left I could talk to anyway." Whether that was true or not, he had always been a man of few words, and he lived his life largely in solitude.

The Herrod farm lay between his shack and the town, so he often passed by and had developed an acquaintance with Dickey and Gus. Sometimes he would drop off an extra rabbit when he had been lucky and caught more than he could use or sell. Dickey and Gus in turn shared some of whatever alcohol they had. Drinking was Cadman's downfall; he had little resistance to it and could often be seen weaving his way back home after spending whatever was left of his earnings on cheap wine. "It's a miracle that poor man doesn't get run over," Ted's mom had remarked on more than one occasion when they passed him weaving along the margin of the road. All in all, though, he was a gentle man who stayed out of other people's lives—which was the reason he got along with Dickey and Gus. Most everybody spoke politely to Mr. Oliver even as they pitied him and looked down on his lowly status in the community. It was a sad thing to be the last of any group—you could see as much in his face.

The whole proud and unfortunate history of his people seemed to be written there. Wanting nothing more than to be left in peace, he endured.

Again, Dickey invited him in. "C'mon, have a drink."

The boys' eyes were fixed on the newcomer. They watched as he scanned the room, Dickey and Gus, the bottles, the stack of coins, themselves. He went from face to face and surely saw the boys' anxiety, but his own visage gave nothing away. At the end of his sweep, Ted was pained to see the man's eyes return, like a magnet, to the bottles. His right arm lifted and his fingers spread as if to reach out. Then his hand clenched sharply into a fist and dropped back to his side.

"Aw, ma stomach's all screwed up taday, can't keep nothin' down." The hand swung up again, this time to pat his midsection. For emphasis, he shook his head from side to side. Dickey and Gus, having their backs to him, saw nothing of this little pantomime.

"I came cuz I got no tobacco," he said.

So preoccupied were Dickey and Gus with their drinking that they had completely forgotten they also smoked. Being reminded of another pleasure they could abuse, Gus rummaged in the drawer of the table and came up with a small bag of stale Bull Durham and some rolling papers. They passed the "fixins" around, and each man rolled a cigarette in his own characteristic way. Gus worked with almost childlike glee, producing a hurried, twisted, sloppy little thing. Dickey, with grim determination, took most of the pouch and two papers to roll a blunt, fat cigarette as big around as his little finger. Cadman, with the trembling hands of someone who really needed a smoke, took what tobacco was left and shaped a remarkably neat white tube. Dickey raised the chimney from the lamp on the table and they each lit up, sucking in the oily flame. Smoke swirled in the updraft of heat, and a moment of satisfaction seemed to settle over the three men. Gus teased the boys, "Smokin's bad fa ya, ya know," as he drew greedily on his gnarled effort.

"Well, have a seat anyways," insisted Dickey.

Mr. Oliver pulled a chair over, facing the boys but away from the table. As he sat down, he wrung his hands once and then clasped his knees with a deliberateness that told anyone who was looking that he was fighting some strong urge. He drew hard on his cigarette, and the ember flared brightly. The other two men, whose chins were sinking closer to the table by the minute, didn't notice that set of gestures either.

Dickey roused himself. "You know somethin' about my old man movin' bootlegger liquor through here, don't ya?" Ted could tell Dickey considered Cadman a person of little consequence and was comfortable revealing his story to him.

"Some, not much."

"Did ya know 'bout the shipment that gut sunk?"

"No."

"Well, one time, this whole boatload goes down outside Frenchman's Cove, hit the ledge or sumpthin'. Those hoods from Providence were mad as hell, gave ol' Carl a hard time, pushed him around a bit for some reason. He didn't have nothing ta do with the boat, though. Carl, a'course, passed a little of their grief on to me and my ma, so I remember it good." At this Dickey drifted off, lost in thought for a moment. "Well, anyways," he snapped to, "nobuddy remembers 'bout it but me, till these punks found it. There's even slot machines. Tomorra we're gonna go back and get what's left." He riffled the stack of silver dollars. As an afterthought, he shot a look toward the bed and added, "Then they're gonna keep their mouths shut, ain't ya?"

"That's a pretty big secret ta keep," said Gus.

"They'll keep it if they know what's good for 'em," snarled Dickey.

He stood up unsteadily, braced himself against the fireplace, reached back into the shadows, and pulled out a double-barreled shotgun, which he laid across the table, pointing the muzzle in the direction of the boys. From the mantle he grabbed a box of shells and set it down with an emphatic thump. He flopped back into his seat, cracked open the gun, put in two bright green shells, and then snapped it closed. This time he angled the barrels in the general direction of the stove.

"They keep their mouths shut, they gut no problem," he said.

As this bit of drama settled over the room, Dickey and Gus began to drink again. In a while, Zolly began to fidget.

"Whatsa matter?" Gus grumbled.

"I gotta pee," said Zolly in a pleading voice, "real bad."

Dickey looked at Gus. "Take 'im out an watch 'im," Dickey ordered.

Gus, almost too drunk to stand, looked at Cadman and said, "You take 'im."

"Ain't watchin' nobody," said the other man.

"Aw, go piss in the sink," Gus whined.

"Ya do that?" Dickey blurted in disgust.

"Well, sometimes, only when it's really cold, ya know," Gus said in a sniveling voice, making an effort to squirm out of the hole he'd just stepped in.

For no other reason than it was easier than bullying Gus or Cadman, Dickey allowed it: "Okay, kid, use the sink." Even this small concession to normal bodily needs seemed to irritate him. It was obvious that this was not the way he had imagined events working out when the evening began.

Zolly pointed to the rope still around his neck.

Gus grunted, forced himself up, and went over to the bed. He fumbled with the knot for a bit and then told Buzzy to untie it. Once freed, Zolly went to the back of the room, unzipped, and stood on his tiptoes. The sink was a bit high. The room became silent; everybody waited. Thirty seconds, a minute went by. Zolly stood there.

"Come on, kid," Dickey groused.

"I can't," Zolly whined.

"Siddown then," Dickey said with growing irritation.

"But I gotta go," persisted Zolly. Everybody watching and waiting had him locked up tight.

Dickey exploded in rage. Overcoming his stupor, he threw back his chair, strode across the room, grabbed Zolly by the shoulder, and spun him around. Wide-eyed and gap-mouthed, Zolly stared into the big man's furious face. The two stood frozen for a moment, and then, at the same instant, they both realized that Zolly had finally let go and was peeing all over Dickey's pants. Again there was a bellow, as if he had been stabbed. Dickey's beefy hands shot out to slam Zolly into the back wall, and the boy slid to the floor still spouting urine between his splayed legs.

"Aagh, aagh." Dickey turned to the room, the front of his pants dark with wetness.

Gus was straining to suppress laughter. Ted and Buzzy were frozen in anticipation of what might happen next. Luckily, even rough guys like Dickey don't want to deal with anything like pee.

Without another word, he dragged Zolly up on his feet and almost threw him back toward the bed. He then went into the shadows of the far corner and, after some shuffling, returned to the table wearing an identical pair of blue work pants—if anything, dirtier and more wrinkled than the previous pair.

"Anybuddy else need ta piss?" he asked.

The others shook their heads. Then Dickey and Gus began to drink again. After a while, Gus ducked under the table and came up with, of all things, a box of Devil Dogs.

"Fell off a garbage truck," he joked as he tore the cellophane from one of the cream-filled devil's-food fingers and began to eat.

After a few bites, he decided that the pastry was "still good" and threw one to each boy. The wrapping did smell a bit odd, and though it made the boys feel like trained seals, the simple activity of catching, opening, and eating helped break the intolerable tension that had built up. Cadman Oliver went over and took himself one of the mass-produced confections, and the six of them sat there for a while munching away.

Ted soon noticed that Gus hadn't bothered to tie Zolly in again, and it dawned on him that having more mobility might help if things got really bad. He signaled with his eyes, and the other boys nodded back in recognition. He also noticed that Zolly was fumbling with something behind his back. Zolly himself had just discovered that the stone knife was still rolled in the waistband of his shorts where he had hidden it after he changed clothes. When he had freed it, he nudged Buzzy and passed the blade to him. If the other boy was surprised or puzzled, he didn't show a thing. With Dickey and Gus distracted eating Devil Dogs between swallows of rum, Ted quickly caught on and made a bend in the rope, forming a loop. He then held firm as Buzzy pulled against it with the ancient edge. Sawing through a half inch of cotton rope was not an easy thing to manage, especially behind their backs. Buzzy paused for a moment to relax his fingers, and Ted looked up from his concentration directly into the fixed stare of Cadman Oliver. A chill washed over him. Buzzy instantly picked up on his tension. They both froze. Slowly, almost imperceptibly, the old man nodded his head once.

They breathed a small sigh of relief and went back to work. The ancient knife was sharp enough and soon parted the anchor line. Ted worked the cut ends around his left side, exposing them to Cadman Oliver's line of sight. A slow blink and a hint of a nod were the only acknowledgment he got. *What now?*

wondered Ted, as Buzzy passed the knife back to Zolly. Soon, Dickey and Gus began making a commotion, opening the second bottle. Once again, their improvised method surprised dimwitted Gus and squirted booze up into his face. Again he giggled foolishly. "Gin," he pronounced. Again Dickey made Gus take the first drink, but this time Dickey couldn't control his compulsion more than a few seconds before he grabbed the bottle and filled his own glass. Ted was really rooting for poison this time—fast-acting poison. Gus was somehow mellowing as his drunkenness progressed, slowing him down and making him more lethargic. Dickey, on the other hand, seemed to be getting more agitated. At times, his eyes darted around the room, and yet they didn't seem to focus on anything. His mouth was moving, and he was whispering as if he were talking to someone. The words *haunted* and *crazy* came into Ted's mind. What scared Ted most, though, was Dickey's right hand, which rested on the grip of the shotgun. The index finger absentmindedly stroked the trigger, while his thumb traced slow circles around the safety. Something was coming to a head. Ted looked pleadingly toward Cadman Oliver, who calmed him with a small downward gesture of his palm. All the boys saw it. It said, simply, *Sit tight.*

In a second, Cadman cleared his throat and stood up. "Gotta piss," he said, "and I ain't doin' it in no sink." At the door he turned, signaled with his chin toward the French windows at the front of the room, and repeated the hand sign.

Ted looked over at the windows. Like everything else about the house, they were in disrepair. Several panes of glass were missing and had been replaced with sheets of rusted tin. The frames were coming apart at the joints. The windows were also nailed shut. There was no way out in that direction.

Minutes added up. Ted began to wonder if they had been

abandoned. Maybe Cadman Oliver had gone for help, maybe he just left. Eventually, Gus noticed his absence.

"Where'n hell's the Injun?" he asked.

"Maybe he's bein' sick," answered Dickey.

"Maybe he's dead," retorted Gus.

"He betta come back or he will be dead," threatened Dickey.

Moments later, they heard heavy footsteps on the porch and then a thump as if a weight had been set down. Ted caught a flash of something large and white outside the window an instant before a long section of one of the porch columns came plunging through the French doors like a tree toppling over. It angled in, showering glass and splintered wood all over the boys, who threw up their arms to protect themselves as it crashed to the floor at their feet, leaving a black hole out into the night. Dickey was so startled he jumped up and knocked over the table. Everything went flying: the bottles, the lamp, the gun, the coins, the Devil Dogs. The next thing the boys knew, Cadman Oliver was standing next to them, pushing them toward the new exit. In a clear, firm voice he said, "Go! Straight across the porch toward the barn." Ted and Buzzy were through the opening in a flash, but several tumbled boxes had blocked Zolly's path. He hesitated a moment, long enough for Gus to reach over the fallen table and grab his arm. Without thinking, Zolly pivoted and, in a roundhouse swing, drove the stone blade into Gus's forearm. Despite the confusion of the moment, Zolly felt a flood of satisfaction in the act. He also felt the point striking bone and twisting sideways before there was a slight snap. The tip had broken off in Gus's arm. The man yowled in pain and fell back. Zolly sprung out across the porch.

When the table went over, the lamp had smashed against the stove, igniting the spilled oil with its own flame. Blocked by the fire from rounding the table in the direction, of the stove, Dickey started around the other end. Cadman flung a chair at him and then overturned the bed, blocking a path to the open window as he escaped into the dark.

Out in the yard, the boys were standing together. As Cadman came up, they turned to flee but he halted them. "Wait!" Stepping around in front of them, he spread his arms and turned them back to face the house. Ted's brain was screaming, *Run, run, let's run! Why are we waiting?* It must have taken only a minute, but it seemed like a year before Dickey's outline appeared against the orange glow of the hallway, bright from the spreading flames. He didn't pause a second before he charged like a bull out the front door, the shotgun held high across his chest. Ted could only think *It's over for us, right now. We're dead for sure, dead!* But when Dickey reached the top step, one of his legs seemed to halt in midstride, and his body pitched forward straight at them. In a split second, he was horizontal. *Like a blimp,* thought Ted, *sailing silently through the air.* One of Dickey's cuffs had gotten splashed with oil from the lamp and was on fire. He trailed a short flame. Though he may have looked weightless for an instant, he quickly succumbed to the pull of gravity, crashing to the dusty ground like a side of meat. Right on his heels, Gus emerged from the burning house at a trot. He barely got "Dickey" out of his mouth before he too took a queer hitched step and tumbled through the air. His fall wasn't as severe, since he landed on top of the big man.

"Behind the barn," whispered Cadman. They now turned and ran.

What he had done in his absence "ta piss" was locate a length of fence wire and tie it, about a foot up, between the columns on either side of the front step. Holding the boys in place was the only way he could be sure that Dickey would come straight off the porch and not veer left or right, missing the trip wire. With any luck, Dickey might be out of commission; at least he couldn't be sure which way they went.

Rounding the corner of the barn at a run, Ted wasn't

paying attention to the tail of rope trailing from his neck. It rasped along the angle of the shabby structure and wedged into a split in one of the old boards. When it hit a knot, Ted was jerked off his feet, coming down on his back. The ground was a grassy slope; luckily he didn't hit too hard. Buzzy, who was right behind, grabbed the jammed rope on the fly and, with his full weight, tore it free of the weathered board. He and Zolly helped Ted up, and the three stumbled around behind the barn. Ted had the wind knocked out of him but was unhurt except for a nasty rope burn at his throat. When he had recovered a bit, Cadman asked, "You awright?"

"Yah," said Ted in a phlegmy voice. He wouldn't notice the burn until later.

Cadman then produced his own knife and carefully cut the ropes from Ted and Buzzy. While he did this, he asked, "How'd ya get here?"

"Boat from Skunk Island ta Lakeside," coughed Ted. "We walked from there." Everyone knew the south shore of South Pond as Lakeside.

"Boat still tied there?"

"Yah."

"Big enough for four?"

"Yah."

"Oars?"

"Yah."

"That's where we head then," concluded Cadman. If they got to a rowboat, there was no way the two men could catch them in the scow, and the lake would take them safely all the way to town.

"They made us come here," Buzzy said, with the kind of emphasis that implied it was something a rescuer would need to know. Cadman didn't respond. He was too busy planning their next move. They could already hear voices. Apparently

Dickey hadn't broken his neck. In fact, his smoldering pants leg had roused him with pain.

"Follow me, and stay close," whispered Cadman as he stepped off, directly away from the barn.

They couldn't see the house but, from the shadow that the barn was throwing on the trees behind it, they knew it must be burning furiously. They walked in the cover of that shadow directly to a wall about fifty feet out, and then headed east. Cadman whispered over his shoulder, "We follow this to the trolley tracks." They hadn't gotten much out of the shadow when they heard a dull popping sound from the house.

The cases of Sterno had heated up enough to blow their lids, and the cans were spewing jellied alcohol into the conflagration, causing the flames to flare. Mr. Oliver had hoped to sneak away in the shadows of the overhanging trees, but in the bright light the four of them were now plainly visible.

CHAPTER 10

The Chase

"There they are," cried Gus, pointing left of the barn at the line of running figures.

From where the boys were, Gus and Dickey were visible too. Against the flaming house they were small black figures gesturing wildly and darting back and forth as if mad with confusion. Ted thought they looked like the little demons in the "Night on Bald Mountain" part of *Fantasia*.

Suddenly there was a bright muzzle flash, and in a second a rush of birdshot tore up the weeds just feet behind Buzzy, the last in line. Another boom followed almost instantaneously. Somebody yelled, "Run!" and they all took off, sprinting at top speed as the next blast arrived. This time it hit the ground, low and short, kicking up a spray of debris and spent pellets that peppered the middle of their line. Ted felt something like a beesting on his ankle and another weaker strike through his jeans on his calf.

"Yow!" he heard Zolly exclaim.

That's two, thought Ted. *Maybe that's all he's got.* Unfortunately, Dickey had been able to find a dozen shells before the flames drove him from the house. In the time it took him to reload, the group was about out of range of a shotgun. They were passing behind a stand of sumac when they heard the next blast. The pellets now took longer to reach them and fell as harmless as rain on the broad leaves of the plants. By the fourth shot, Dickey was firing blind, and nothing came down within their hearing. They kept running for another hundred yards and then stopped to reconnoiter. "Anybuddy hit?" puffed Mr. Oliver. Zolly had a nasty welt on his cheek. Ted felt a similar one on his ankle, but he didn't take the time to pull up his pant leg and check there. Through the leaves, they could still see Dickey and Gus at the house, arguing about something. That ended abruptly when Dickey stormed off downhill in their direction. Gus trailed along behind, cradling his injured arm.

With Mr. Oliver in the lead, they again took off. There was no path, and three stone walls joined the one they followed, slowing their flight. "Careful for the barbed wire," cautioned Mr. Oliver as they felt their way over the first. They were in darkness again. Bushes in the overgrown field blocked the light from the intensely burning house, where flames were now coming out of the second-floor windows, consuming the porch roof. Burning tar was dripping into the dry grass that grew right up against the foundation. The second stone wall was painfully slow to get over. If Dickey took the old cart road, as was likely, he would be gaining on them. The third wall was the one at the railbed. Ted wondered if Dickey had gotten there ahead of them. Was he waiting to ambush them as they crossed? Mr. Oliver signaled for quiet. Their location had a view north, up the trolley bed to where the cart road came out. They waited. It was too much of a risk to attempt a run for the other side. If Dickey were waiting, they would be easy targets. When enough time had elapsed that they could be sure that Dickey had at least reached the barway, Mr. Oliver signaled for them to move north in the cover of the wall. As quietly as they could, they crept forward.

A northerly breeze had come up and would help muffle any noise they made. It would also carry Dickey's sound to them. At the moment, the same wind was fanning flames through the dry grass toward the barn. About halfway to the cart road, they heard footsteps and fell to the ground, hugging the wall. The steps were slow and regular, not the halting, uneven stride of a drunk. It seemed rage and adrenalin had sobered Dickey up. As they lay there panting, too terrified to move, the mosquitoes had free access to any exposed skin. Agonizingly, Ted could hear the buzzing as they landed on his one exposed ear, but he didn't dare move a muscle to swat the bugs away. They were all bitten mercilessly as it took Dickey several long minutes to walk down to the juncture of the two walls. They lay silently, now holding their breath, as he climbed the banking and walked along the wall for a few feet. He obviously knew where they had been headed. Whatever else he was, Dickey had a reputation for being a good hunter, and he knew this area well. It was fortunate that Mr. Oliver had them move. It was also a good thing that Dickey didn't have any kind of light, or he might have been able to spot signs of their having been there, or searched more thoroughly. They heard him pass close by again. When they felt he would be far enough away, they peeked over the wall and could just make out the shadows of two men arguing again. That ended when Dickey gave Gus a shove back up the tracks in the direction they had marched earlier with the boys.

"Must be goin' ta the boat," whispered Mr. Oliver. "Might sit there all night." It was obvious; the safest thing they could do was to head in the opposite direction. If they went back to the farm, the fire department might eventually arrive—but so might Dickey and Gus. They all knew that the railbed crossed over Windham Road at a trestle about two miles south. Surely with the fire there would be traffic passing, and they could flag down help. They waited a long ten minutes and then climbed over the wall and headed south.

Almost immediately, they heard fast-moving footsteps behind them. Dickey and Gus had not gone to the boat, but had waited for them to come out into the open. Fortunately, the railbed veered left here, so Dickey didn't immediately have a clear shot from where he and Gus had been hiding. When he rounded the curve, they would be in his sights again. Mr. Oliver plunged into the woods on the east side of the track. The boys barreled in after him. With no path, they crashed through the grabbing, scraping undergrowth. Had he been alone, Cadman Oliver could have lost Dickey in a minute, but with three boys in tow that was doubtful. Breathing deeply, he halted and indicated southeast with his hand. "Go straight a half mile, you'll come to a ledge. Wait on the far side, in the shadows; I'll pick you up. We double back to the boat." As he left them, he stripped off his dark jacket to reveal a white T-shirt beneath. Even in the weak light under the trees, he was plainly visible. He was going to try to draw Dickey away in another direction.

The boys hadn't gotten far when they heard a shotgun blast, and their hearts sunk. *Perhaps,* Ted thought grimly, *we're on our own again.* They continued on a straight line and eventually came to the top of the ledge. They heard another blast, further away this time, and somehow that gave them encouragement. It was a difficult climb down. In the shadows at the base, Ted couldn't help but notice how similar the spot was to where the "lady's" bones rested. *How long,* he wondered, *had humans sought shelter in places like this?* They hunched in silence, watching the moon rise through the trees as they swatted mosquitoes.

At first, the events of the last few hours just washed over them in a jumble of vivid, disjointed impressions. Ted kept hearing Gus's cackle and seeing Dickey Herrod's blank eyes, the flaming house, the column crashing through the window. Though his heart rate was returning to normal, he could still feel his pulse thumping in his ears. As a distraction, he tried to recall the plot of the movie *The Most Dangerous Game,* in which the villain makes a sport of hunting Joel McCray and some girl on a private jungle island. Ted thought it might be of use if he could remember how the hero had managed to get out of that situation, but right then he couldn't.

He fingered his ankle. It wasn't wet with blood. The skin didn't seem broken. When the swelling went down, it would probably be no more than a nasty bruise. The lump on his calf felt the same, and the fabric of his jeans hadn't been penetrated. For the first time he noticed the chafed skin burning under his chin, but that was too raw to even touch with his salty, sweaty hands. He looked over at Zolly, who was stroking his cheek. "You okay?" Ted whispered. Zolly nodded yes. Buzzy, who was sitting between, reached out and linked hands with them both. It was a firm, dry grip, and Ted was surprised by how satisfying it was to feel the contact. They sat without moving for some time, and then, with a short shake and a parting squeeze, Buzzy let go.

Just then, they heard a coarse whisper from above: "Boys?" It was Mr. Oliver.

Before they could get to their feet, it seemed he was beside them, looking none the worse for wear. He pulled out a red bandana, wiped his face, and blew his nose. Again he asked, "You all awright?"

"Yah," answered Ted, and then he thought to ask, "How 'bout you?"

"I'm okay. With any luck, Dickey thinks we're headed for Windham Road above the farm and is searchin' those fields south of his property. We better go. He's pretty cagey."

The ledge formed a kind of wall roughly parallel to the shore of the swamp some fifty yards away. A well-worn path meandered between the wall and the water's edge. A mile and a half north, it would take them back to Lakeside. They walked in silence but at a quick pace, feeling with each step that they were leaving their pursuers farther behind.

At the point where the ground began to incline and cover the ledge, they first heard and then saw Dickey coming from the opposite direction. He probably figured he had them trapped between the water and the rock wall, so his full concentration was on ranging left and right off the path to check possible hiding places. He hadn't spotted them and couldn't have heard anything over his own noisy tramping. They quietly reversed course, heading back down the path. Past the spot where the boys had hidden earlier, another short trail branched off left toward the swamp and dead-ended in a brushy point of land. Just beyond that junction, they saw Gus standing motionless. Light from the just-risen moon glinted off the blade of the knife that he now held in his left hand.

As they froze, he called out in a loud voice, "I gut 'em … ova here!" He motioned threateningly with the blade. "Come on, I gut a score ta settle," he hissed

If he hadn't had the knife, they would probably have just bowled him over, but Mr. Oliver had another gambit to play. He took the turn down the path toward the water, and the boys followed.

"We gut 'em!" Gus began yelling excitedly. "We gut 'em now!"

At first, Ted thought the same thing; this was a peninsula, cut off on three sides by water. The slender spit of land they were now running along stuck out into the swamp, creating a narrow bottleneck with a corresponding sliver of dry ground that reached out from the other shore. The two points of land were known locally as The Fingers. The group quickly reached the water, and Mr. Oliver barked out, "Go across. Good footing. Dickey's afraid of the swamp. Gravel pit on the other side. Meet up there." Then he literally pushed them through the thick bushes that rimmed the water's edge and splashed in behind.

The bottom was indeed solid. The narrow channel was shallow and there was enough movement to keep the gravel swept clear of mud. As they pulled themselves through the waist-deep water, they could hear the voices of the two men just behind. In a moment, Dickey would have a clear shot. Time slowed. With every step—and, it seemed, every heartbeat—Ted expected to hear an explosion and feel the pellets' impact. He clenched his teeth as he churned forward with agonizing slowness. It was like slogging through maple syrup. He hadn't noticed that Mr. Oliver, last in line, was screening them with his own body. Suddenly, the anticipated blast came, but somehow, it didn't sound like all the others. It was muffled and seemed to go up into the air. No pellets hit the water. Sensing something, they slowed. Mr. Oliver shooed them forward: "Go, go," he said. Buzzy was already at the far shore.

Then they heard Gus cry out in a loud, then louder voice: "Dickey? Dickey!" The long silence that followed ended with a strange catlike yowl and the sound of hurried, stumbling footsteps moving away from the water. They heard the eerie scream one more time as Gus turned south on the main path. They looked at each other questioningly, not knowing what to do. Then a deep-throated moan filled the air. It rose and then seemed to implode and drag all the sounds around them into some deep hole. It was the kind of thing that once heard, you could never forget, and right there Ted hoped to never hear it again.

Mr. Oliver brushed water toward them, indicating that they should climb out on the far side. He himself quietly crept back to where they had come. The opposite shore, where the boys came out of the channel, was strewn with boulders, where they took shelter and waited. It wasn't long before they heard Mr. Oliver's voice: "All clear, come on back."

As they waded back, the moon was over their shoulders, and they could only make out a dark shape in the bushes where they themselves had so recently passed. Around the side of the point was a spot where occasional use by fishermen had created an opening in the brush. From there, looking back toward the channel, they got a view of Dickey's body suspended motionless in the tangled bushes. Framed against the dappling water, he made a bizarre silhouette. The thick blueberry and blackberry branches were stiff enough to support his weight and held him suspended in a grotesque pose, like some giant marionette on invisible strings. With his upper body leaning forward, his head sagged deeply down between his shoulders. His right arm was propped straight out behind him, entangled in the brush, while his left hung down at his side. His right leg was back, the toe of his shoe resting on the shore. His left leg dangled limply in the water. The gun had somehow landed upright in the swamp, and only its twin barrels, one of them smoking, were visible above water. Dickey had somehow shot himself.

They stared dumbstruck at the tableau for some time. Then Mr. Oliver found a stick and used it to reach out and push the gun over, so that it splashed beneath the surface. "Don't think we'll have any more trouble from Gus, but it's best that gun's outa sight." He sighed, shook his head, and added, "Varmints or stray dogs may get at him before the police, but there's nothing we can do now."

Before they turned to go, Mr. Oliver told the boys what he knew about Dickey's fear of the swamp. Dickey had on occasion confessed guilt for abandoning his mother to his father's violent outbursts. He believed that she was buried somewhere in the swamp, and he had recurring nightmares of her rising up from the water and calling him to join her. Mr. Oliver spoke in the hushed monotone of someone reciting a graveside prayer, as if revealing the secret could, in some way, ease the passage of the departed soul. Perhaps the old man thought it was something the boys needed to know, something that might help them understand their ordeal. As they headed down the path, he whispered, "Bless his spirit. Never really had much of a chance in this life." Ted thought this an extraordinarily generous thing to say about a man who had just been trying to kill them.

The walk back to the boat took half an hour. No one spoke along the way. Ted couldn't stop his brain from sorting through events. He was grateful for the rhythm of the marching and brought his heels down with jarring, stiff-legged force in an attempt to shake off some of the terror of the last hours. He assumed the others were also caught up in the same whirlwind of emotions. In a while, the adrenaline rush seemed to drain away with the water dripping from his sodden clothing. The realization that they were finally out of danger allowed Ted to consider some of the alternate possibilities of how events could have gone. He shuddered.

As Ted's fear subsided, anger rose to take its place. Inside he raged at the stupidity of the men who had humiliated and brutalized him and his friends over so little. Couldn't those fools have thought for one second about what they were doing? He hated Dickey for the blindness of his actions. He hated him for his stupidity. He hated him for dying right in front of them. Finally, though, recalling Mr. Oliver's parting benediction, he felt a pang of pity for the man and his sad life. As they walked, the surroundings began to shift back from a place laden with threat to merely night woods lit by a silver moon.

Chapter 11

Reconciled

They towed the scow along to Skunk Island, where they stopped to change clothes. Mr. Oliver looked uncomfortable after donning Buzzy's sweatshirt and jeans, but the night was getting cooler and it was good to be dry. He kept his wet shoes on, and his hat had never gotten a drop on it. Nothing was said about the silver, and they took nothing with them except the tally board. If Mr. Oliver wondered why they would take what appeared to be a greasy old plank, he said nothing. As they pushed off for the row home, they could see an orange glow above the trees in the southwest. The wind had dropped, but the fire had spread out, and the fields around the house were obviously in flames. When they were about midway across the pond, they began to hear distant sirens. Fire companies from three towns were responding, but by this time there was little to do but keep the fast-moving flames from invading the surrounding woods. The firefighters let the house and barn

115

burn themselves out and then doused the ashes. In essence, every physical aspect of the Herrod family was incinerated in one night, though accounts of their story would live on in the town's memory.

The four figures in the slow-moving boat remained locked in thought as they pulled across South Pond. It took nearly an hour to reach Breezy Point Narrows. As they passed through and headed out toward Middle Pond, the air became cooler again, and puffs of mist began to form. As the fog thickened, the idea of rowing all the way into town seemed to evaporate. After all, Mr. Morracy had a phone and a car. As they turned toward the nearby shore, Mr. Oliver made a weak protest: "Don't care to go there." But the logic of heading for the marina was undeniable. As if they hadn't heard him, the boys rowed in and tied up. Being on familiar ground raised their spirits, and they scrambled with newfound energy to be the first to reach Mr. Morracy's house and tell the story. Cadman waited in the boat as the boys dashed off along the shore. Crowding on the front steps, they knocked furiously, rattling the glass in the door. Footsteps sounded, and the outside light came on as Mr. Morracy's groggy face appeared from behind the curtain.

"Boys!" was all he got out. Before he could turn the key and get the door open, they were talking over one another, each throwing out bits of the tale: Frenchman's Cove, sunken boat, whiskey, Indian grave, Dickey Herrod, Cadman Oliver. "Hold on," protested Mr. Morracy. "Cadman Oliver is here?"

"Yah, he's in the boat."

"And you found some sort of Indian gravesite?" Mr. Morracy asked.

"Yah, and, and we found beads and some kinda stone knife and ..."

He cut them short again. "Hold it, have you told Cadman this?"

"No, so much else happened."

"Okay," said Mr. Morracy, blinking himself awake and clutching the collar of his pajamas up under his chin. "Go on."

They finished their tale in broad strokes, telling him about their march through the woods, the house, the terrifying run, the fire. When they got to Dickey's death, they could see Mr. Morracy react with shock.

"Dickey's dead?" he asked in disbelief.

"Yah, we better call the cops, huh?" said Ted, thinking that maybe it was time to get professionals involved.

"Yes … yes," said Mr. Morracy, and he turned to go for the phone. Halfway there, he paused. "But let's go down to the shop first," he said thoughtfully.

He threw on a jacket and slipped into a pair of work shoes as they headed back to the boathouse. The rowboat sat motionless in the dark water. Cadman Oliver was still hunched in the same spot on the front thwart.

"Hello, Cadman," said Oscar Morracy as they came up. Cadman Oliver said nothing.

"Tell 'im the part about the burial site," Mr. Morracy directed Ted.

Oscar Morracy and Cadman Oliver had a long association, and they were friends before the boys were born. They had hunted and fished together for years, but that ended in bitterness when the gravel rights to Breezy Point were sold. There had always been a strange clearing on the rise, overlooking the lake at the eastern tip of the peninsula. In fifty feet of flat, open ground, seven slabs of rough shale were set upright in two uneven rows. There were no other large pieces of that type of stone nearby, so the general conclusion was that someone had moved them there and set them up. Not surprisingly, they were known as the Indian Graves, even though sporadic digging had uncovered no remains or artifacts.

To most people, the stones were simply a puzzlement. To Cadman Oliver, they were a physical link to his ancestral past. Whether his assumption was correct or not, they were, in his native tongue, *Chaboken* ("Place of the Separated")—sacred ground. When the mining for gravel began, Cadman had extracted a promise from his friend Oscar that the point would be spared. Nonetheless, Cadman watched nervously as the steam shovel crept forward and the landmass trickled away a truckload at a time. In the second year of the excavation, the great shovel was getting too close to the stones. He had seen the pattern before: slow encroachment on the ruins of a sweat lodge or a burial ground surrounded by cornfields. Then one day, when no one was looking, they were gone, as if they had never been—plowed under, planted over, built on. Even those who sympathized with him would shrug and say, "There's nothing you can do now, Cadman. What's done's done. Ya can't put it back."

With courage stoked by desperation, Cadman decided he would make a stand this time. One night in late summer, he camped out on the steam shovel so as to be there when the workers arrived in the morning. Unfortunately, he had brought a bottle along to keep him company, and at dawn when the trucks rolled in he was a bit incoherent. It didn't help that he threw what little Nipmuck he knew into his speech. Words like *Napasooenegg* ("at the Upright Stones") and *Cowasset* ("the Place of Pines") went right over the heads of the Italian and Greek immigrants who worked for the cement company. Cadman didn't actually speak his own language. Most of the words that had filtered down to him were place names, but just forming them in his mouth and hearing them spoken out loud gave him heart.

The only thing clear to the workmen was that Cadman didn't intend to move. Three of them approached, ready to drag him from where he sat on the massive iron tread, but Cadman produced a knife. The men weren't being paid to deal with threats like that, so the senior Mr. Morracy was called. Oscar came along.

"Well, couldn't ya just leave this last bit?" Cadman pleaded.

"No," the men said. They had orders. The owner of the cement company was called. Commitments had been made; it wasn't the money, that sand was needed now. The Morracys had signed a contract. They had better honor it.

By nine o'clock, a single police cruiser arrived, and as Officer Chesler unfolded his six-foot-two frame from the driver's seat, Cadman's resolve faded. Police Corporal Chesler had considerable experience dealing with drunks. Doing so was kind of his specialty. Cadman himself was an old acquaintance, having spent many nights "sleeping one off" in a jail cell at the station. The outcome of this interaction was now a foregone conclusion. With a world-weary look on his face, Officer Chesler listened to the workmen, letting them vent a bit before he put up his hands in a gesture of peace and slowly approached Cadman. As he got closer, Cadman made one halfhearted swipe at him with the knife, but faster than anyone could see from twenty feet away, he was in a hammerlock and the handcuffs were being put on. As Cadman was loaded into the backseat of the police car, he looked pleadingly at his friend Oscar, who stood there mute. Not wanting to deal with the complications of paperwork, Officer Chesler assured everyone, "He won't be back. I'll keep an eye on 'im. Don't worry."

On the drive back to town, the kindly policeman delivered his, "Ya just can't fight the law, Cadman" lecture. In the long run, he didn't even bother to book Cadman, and after a day and a night in jail Cadman walked out the door so meekly that it moved even Steve Chesler's heart. By that time, the Indian Graves had been flattened. What was done was done. Cadman's spirit had been stepped on one more time; he had again failed to carry the burden of his people, and a friend had betrayed him. There was not much more the world could do. He had never been back to Breezy Point until this night.

><

"Go on, tell 'im," repeated Mr. Morracy as they stood there on the dock. Ted went through the events again, being careful to skip over the part about moving the skull. When he got to the stone knife, Zolly bent down and put it in Cadman Oliver's hands like some ritual object. "I'm sorry it's broke," he whispered. "The tip must be in Gus's arm. He grabbed me when I was running out, and I used it." To hear that the ancient blade had actually struck a blow in his lifetime lifted Cadman spirits.

"That's okay, I'm sure whoever made this would be glad it helped ya," he said as he studied the knife.

The others gave him their shell beads. There was a long pause. Then Cadman simply looked up with tears in his eyes and said, "Thank you."

With Mr. Morracy's prodding, Ted finished the story with a detailed description of the sunken burial site.

"Soon as this gets out, there's gonna be people an' divers all over that place," said Mr. Morracy. "They'll find it for sure. Come with me," he said bluntly as he pivoted on his heal military-style and headed up the steps to his office.

Unlocking the door, he pulled down the shade on the big window, turned on the lights, waved Ted over to the desk, and pushed a pad and pencil in front of him. "Draw me a map of the cove. Show me where this boat 'n' grave's at," he instructed.

As the features of the drawing emerged, he hung over Ted's shoulder, keeping pace with questions. "How far from the shore to here, the wall? How high is it? How deep's the cove in the middle? Can you guide the *Lady* in there?" When Ted began drawing a cross-section of the ledge and the shelf where the body lay, Mr. Morracy kept up the drumbeat of his inquiry. "How high off the bottom is she?" Then, pointing with his finger, he asked, "How does the wall slope there? How deep's the overhang? What's the bottom like here?"

When he got his answers, Mr. Morracy straightened up, stroked his chin, and pursed his lips. Then, with a deliberateness and authority none of them had ever seen before, he began to issue orders. The place came alive with activity. Ted was sent to retrieve a pair of massive rusted roof hooks that for as long as he could remember had hung on the rim of an old oil barrel out in the weeds. The two question-mark-shaped arcs of steel were about eighteen inches long, with a strong eyelet on the short straight end and a deep sweeping C hook on the other. They looked like fishhooks that were all hook and no shank. Mr. Morracy had borrowed them to anchor scaffolding during the construction of the boathouse and had never bothered to return them. Now it appeared they were intended for some new use. When Ted got back, the office was empty except for Mr. Oliver, who was standing at the door looking into the bay. Ted climbed down the steep stairs, and Mr. Oliver passed him the hooks. Mr. Morracy was just then directing Zolly to retrieve some heavy rope stored in the rafters over the office. When two big coils were thrown down, Buzzy was put to work tying one end of each to the eyelet of the hooks. Ted was pointed to the rear seats of the boat and told to make two rope nests with a hook on top of each. Mr. Morracy himself climbed aboard and opened the engine doors to check the bilge. Ted's caulking from earlier in the week had held; there would be no need to bail.

When Mr. Morracy looked up, Cadman's questioning face caught his eye.

"Ya ain't gonna to try ta move her, are ya?" asked Cadman.

"No, don't worry," said Mr. Morracy confidently. "We won't touch her at all. We're gonna cover her deeper. They'll neva find 'er. They'll neva even think ta look. With all that other stuff out there, they're gonna be lookin' for metal. She's gonna be awright." Exactly how this task would be accomplished was, at the moment, a mystery to everyone but Oscar Morracy.

Work proceeded at a brisk pace. Mr. Morracy pulled a large searchlight from a storage cabinet and fitted its stanchion into a socket just ahead of the windshield on the driver's side of the boat. Then he stretched out the cord, plugged it into the receptacle for the cigarette lighter, and flipped the switch. A shaft of intense light stabbed up into the rafters. He twisted a knob that controlled the focus of the beam, cranking it in to about ten feet, and then swiveled the whole apparatus so that its hot white light shot down into the water. He switched the light off and called for two large oars to be passed onboard. With those stowed in the midsection, he started the blower and turned the key. The engine jolted to life. He revved it once and then let it settle back to a rumbling idle, belching bubbles from the exhaust port.

"Okay, let's go," he said from behind the wheel. "Get the lights and open the bay doors."

Mr. Oliver took care of the office lights and then climbed down the stairs. Ted pulled the switch in the bay as the other boys pushed the huge wooden doors out. When the doors had swung around and banged against the outside wall, Mr. Morracy began to ease the *Lady* out. Ted and Mr. Oliver climbed onboard as she slid from her berth. Zolly and Buzzy were instructed to pull the doors closed behind and then hustle around through the office to the dock.

"Don't want anybody knowin' we're out ... and lock the office door on your way," Mr. Morracy called after them.

At a steady idle, the huge dark shape eased to the fueling dock, where Buzzy and Zolly hopped on. Then, at low throttle, Mr. Morracy swung the boat around and headed for the narrows. A mist was building and visibility was poor. Ted looked over at Mr. Morracy, who was grinning from ear to ear. Apparently conditions suited him just fine. Emerging onto South Pond, he opened her up, and they were in front of Frenchman's Cove before the damp wind had a chance to give any of them a chill. The shallow water of the little bay produced only a faint haze, and they could see the shore quite well. In the last few days, the boys had become familiar with the underwater topography, so with the aid of the searchlight, they quickly spotted the high point of the ledge and the section of wall where Whitfield Duffy and the smugglers had bottomed out. The lady, the first Lady of the Lake, lay near the bottom about ten yards south of there.

They located a crack in the ledge and fished one of the big roof hooks into it. Zolly and Buzzy, each with an oar in hand, stood ready to push off if they drifted too close to the rocks. They then moved ten yards to the other side of the burial location, paying out line as they went. Now sixty feet from the first hook, they found a sharp edge of rock to catch with the second hook. Mr. Morracy then carefully maneuvered behind the wall into the cove and centered the boat between the hooks. He pointed the bow to shore and crept forward as Ted and Buzzy kept tension on the trailing lines sliding out through their hands. What they were doing was creating a giant steep-sided triangle, the base of which was the sixty feet of ledge and wall. The sloping sides of the triangle were the ropes. The apex was at the boat. When they were some twenty feet from shore, the rope ran out. Mr. Morracy tied the two ends to the heavy chrome ringbolt that he had installed to pull water skiers, and then he hooked the ropes around jam cleats on either side of the craft near the stern.

"Okay," he whispered. "Let's give it a try."

He slid back into the cockpit and advanced the throttle. The boat moved toward shore a few feet and stopped as the ropes tightened. The prop was still churning, but their forward motion was halted. As Mr. Morracy nudged the throttle forward again, increasing the motor's RPMs, the ropes tightened and the bow lifted a bit from the thrust of the propeller, but they held steady in place. With the searchlight swiveled toward the stern, everyone could see clouds of muddy water being pushed out by the prop wash.

So that was Mr. Morracy's idea—to use the propeller to blow the bottom of Frenchman's Cove out over the wall, where it could rain down along the foot of the ledge. As Ted was coming to this realization, the throttle got kicked up another notch. The whole boat shook with the rush of power, the ropes strained, and brown water darker than rapids on the Colorado River churned out behind. Mr. Morracy still had a grin plastered on his face. When he throttled up again, they began to hear pebbles pinging off the blades of the prop, and he quickly eased back. They had obviously blown all the mud clear from immediately underneath them and were now sucking up gravel. Thirty feet of rope was quickly hauled in and retied. They repeated the procedure. This time, because the water was deeper, they almost redlined the tachometer before they cut back on the RPMs. Within a half hour they had repeated the procedure three times and were getting closer to the wall. In the process, Mr. Morracy discovered that he could direct the growing plume of mud by swinging the rudder left and right, subtly shifting the angle of their thrust. In an hour, they were almost at the wall, now pushing so much mud that it was slower going. They were, however, heartened by the amount of swirling, sludgy water they saw boiling over the shallow spot above the wall. In the open lake beyond, the energy of their thrust quickly dissipated, and the silt seemed to settle straight down ... mostly. A vast brown soup now surrounded them inside the cove. There was no way to calculate exactly how much solid matter had been washed over the wall, but they knew it must be a lot. They hauled in one more time. The ropes seemed to reach almost straight from the sides at this point, but the hooks held firm. At low power, Mr. Morracy attempted to "dust off" the wall, "so's it don't look too strange. Anyway," he concluded, "most folks in town don't know what the bottom looks like out here. By the time anyone in the know has a look-see, there'll of been so many fools about stirring things up that it won't make no difference."

They motored around to the lake and retrieved the hooks. "Knew I'd find those things handy one day," joked Mr. Morracy. It was still an hour before dawn, and the fog was at its peak. He cruised up and down a couple of times parallel to the wall. "Get some wave action goin'. Wash down a little of the mud on this side," he said. His final move was to point the stern right at the ledge and floor the gas. "Hold on!" he cried merrily as the force of acceleration threw them all back into their seats. At full speed, Mr. Morracy steered a sweeping turn north and then cut back to a slow steady pace.

"Not likely, but there might be some fishermen out here," he said, switching on the running lights. He then instructed the boys to wind the ropes around the hooks. It was slow work that ended up with two objects looking like giant curled-up caterpillars. When they had crept through the narrows and got close to the entrance of the marina, they dropped the hooks and rope into the shallows near the mouth of the lagoon. "Case there's someone waitin' for us up the boathouse," said Mr.

Morracy. He then cut the engine completely. As they drifted, he turned around in his seat and rested his arms on the deck just behind. In his matter-of-fact way, he said, "This whole story hangs together pretty well without the part 'bout that burial site and what we just did. There's no reason that shouldn't stay a secret forever. That lady down there deserves to rest in peace." They all agreed.

CHAPTER 12

Tell It ... Tell It Again

Dawn was breaking as they paddled the last hundred yards around to the boathouse. Mr. Morracy opened the doors over the motor as he rehearsed a story in case there was someone there. "Tried ta get the boys' stuff over at Skunk Island but the *Lady* was actin' up; had ta paddle back. Took for-ever," he said out loud with a wink. The precaution proved unnecessary. They docked and pulled the doors closed. Ted lit a fire for coffee while Buzzy went into the shop for the first-aid kit.

The town of Windham where the Herrod farm was located had no police department of its own, so the Connecticut State Police had jurisdiction there. The sunken boat, on the other hand, was well inside Massachusetts, and the Slaterville police would have sway there. Mr. Morracy decided to make only one call to the local police and let the two authorities sort it out. He kept it brief, ending with, "Ya can find Dickey's body over by the south side of Cranberry Meadow inlet, ya know, The Fingers. Gus ran off. The three of 'em are here safe with me." He then called each of the boy's houses, waking Ted's and Zolly's mothers. There was no answer at Buzzy's; his grandmother's English was so poor that she never touched the phone. All three fathers had taken the family cars to work, so there was no one available to pick up the boys. "Don't worry, they're all fine, I'll bring 'em home myself. The police might wanna talk to 'em," he said in his most comforting voice, and then he passed the phone to Ted.

Ted's mom, after determining that he was all right, wanted to talk to Buzzy. She told him she would walk over to his house and let his grandmother know. "Yah, yah, I'm okay, don't worry, Mrs. S.," said Buzzy, sounding like someone not comfortable with being fussed over yet still appreciating the attention.

With that done, they realized that they were hungry, so the boys went back to the house to see what they could find. Ten minutes later, they returned with what they had scrounged from Mr. Morracy's cupboards as a Slaterville cruiser pulled into the parking lot. It was Chief Stablocki himself. His usually crisp uniform looked as though he had slept in it, his blue policeman's cap was dusted with ash, and he smelled of smoke. It was not unusual for the town police to go over the line into Connecticut, especially when the fire department got called in.

"Mornin', boys," said the chief. "I understand there's more to the fire over at Herrod's place than we know."

"Lots more," responded Ted.

Inside the office, Buzzy was putting bacon in the pan, and the chief had just gotten their names down in his notepad when they heard another car roar into the parking lot and come to a skidding stop that ended with a dull crunch. They all jumped up and went out to see Sergeant Dudley of the Connecticut State Police getting out of his black and white Ford Fairlane, looking a little rattled. He was obviously irritated to see that the local police had arrived ahead of him; he had intended to block in the chief's car, but misjudged his stopping distance on the loose pebbles. To his embarrassment, everyone now stood around gawking at the damage. There wasn't much, really—a taillight, a headlight, and some crumpled chrome—but it was enough to shake his composure. With their broad-brimmed straw hats and dark glasses, state troopers were always supposed to project control.

"We'll deal with this later," Sergeant Dudley said, trying to exert some authority over the situation. "I understand we may be dealing with a homicide here." The word *homicide* was clearly intended to trump everything else.

With seven of them now crowded into the small office, the boys started telling the story again. The room was short on chairs, and Sergeant Dudley stood at the display case for a while before making a fuss and insisting that Mr. Morracy move so he could take over the desk. From his new seat of authority, the sergeant began interrupting the chief's questioning.

Though Mr. Morracy had been rudely displaced in his own office, Ted was surprised to see that he had an amused look on his face as he switched places with the state trooper. In a second, Ted caught on. The conflict between the two police forces was muddling the investigation right here at the outset.

The boys covered the first part of their story quickly without providing much detail. When they told of how Mr. Oliver had pulled them from Dickey's house, the officers paused to look over and acknowledge Cadman for the first time. Up to this point, he had somehow managed to melt into the shadows behind the stove. The boys continued their tale, relating chunks of it in relay as they took turns eating from the frying pan and tending to their wounds. Ted daubed some first-aid cream on his rope burn as he talked. Mr. Morracy cleaned the nasty welt on Zolly's cheek.

The boys didn't try to skip over the money or the hiding place, but they artfully avoided mentioning the trail of jettisoned slot machines that led them to the base of the ledge—and, of course, the lady entombed there. If either of the policemen suspected the boys were holding anything back, he didn't show it. Not knowing much about the speed at which fourteen-year-old boys could move a rowboat, they didn't question the gap in time. And since no one involved was ever questioned separately, they were able to coordinate their stories.

When the boys finished, both officers had their hats off and were scratching their heads. "This is gonna be complicated," admitted Sergeant Dudley. "Abduction across state lines, smuggling, gambling equipment, a fugitive on the run. I'm sure the Mass State Police will get involved, the Alcoholic Beverage Commission, and probably the FBI." The civilians in the room looked at each other in amazement. FBI? Cadman Oliver would later make the observation, "I think my people had considerable fewer problems with the boundaries around here than those folks did."

"Well," said Dudley with a resigned sigh, "we better get over to this Skunk Island and collect your things, before word gets out." Looking at Mr. Morracy, he said, "The chief here and I will take your boat and bring everything back. You can drive these brave lads home now."

"No way," insisted Mr. Morracy. "Ma boat's been actin' up, you'll wind up stranded in the middle-a South Pond. Besides, I know these boys; if they hid sumpthin', they hid it good, and Skunk Island's a bigger place than you think it is."

After some sham tinkering with the *Lady*'s motor and a little bailing, they all piled in and set off.

The officers had to admit that finding the stash would have been harder than they anticipated. When the boys pried up the rock, the four men gaped in amazement at the three rusted cans filled with coins: nearly sixteen pounds of silver. Breaking camp was done quick and sloppy. There would be plenty of time to clean and fold things later. Except for the pile of firewood and Buzzy's grill, nothing was left behind.

Arriving back at the marina, they found Colonel Fenwick and Trooper Nelson of the Massachusetts State Police standing on the dock. They had recovered Dickey's body, and officers from every town in three counties were out looking for Gus. The colonel spoke directly to Chief Stablocki, pointedly snubbing Sergeant Dudley. So it fell to the chief to recount the story as they all stood there on the dock. For some reason, the boys had forgotten to mention the coins that had been on the table just before the fire. When they added that to the telling, Sergeant Dudley went to his car and made a radio call. As the cans were set out on the dock, the colonel, whistling low, and with a false note of regret in his voice, said, "'Fraid I'm gonna hafta take those into evidence."

"Well," said Mr. Morracy, asserting the boys' interests, "they're gonna get counted, and these brave young fellas are gonna get a signed receipt for 'em before they leave their sight."

With mounting impatience, the policemen stood around as the boys counted out nearly fifty stacks of ten coins each and lined them up in neat rows on the office desk. Then, adding to the police officers' irritation, Mr. Morracy insisted that the boys separate the coins into piles by date. "Just in case some of 'em have some extra special value. Ya know how coins are," he said with apparent innocence.

It was nearly eleven a.m. by the time all the counting and signings were completed and Ted was standing with a receipt in hand watching the three police cars drive off. They had used the back side of an old yellowed calendar page, so the document ended up looking a bit like the Declaration of Independence, with all the information at the top and the signatures—including those of Cadman Oliver and Oscar Morracy—scattered randomly around the bottom. It proved to be a very wise thing to have insisted upon. Somehow, though the police literally sifted through the cooling ashes of the house, the other twenty-odd silver coins were never found. "Musta melted er sumpthin'," someone observed. Weeks later, the boys performed an experiment in Ted's fire barrel, and try as they might, they couldn't melt their test piece, a single 1924 Liberty Head silver dollar.

Before Mr. Morracy drove them all home, he made two phone calls: the first to the company that supplied him with gasoline, and the second to Tom Sesnick, the biggest blabbermouth in town.

Chapter 13

What Followed

They transferred their gear to the cavernous trunk of Mr. Morracy's Hudson Hornet, locked up the office, and headed out Breezy Point Road. At State 173, they took a left toward Windham. In five miles, they slowed at a stretch where they could see downhill to the Herrod place. A few fire vehicles remained, stamping out the last pockets of smoldering grass. In the middle of the blackened fields, the foundations of the house and barn seemed tiny, like burnt-out campfires. The gray squares of stone and the dirt road leading in were the only indications that there had ever been buildings there at all.

In another mile and a half, Mr. Morracy slowed again and pulled off to the side. This was the point where the road came closest to Cadman Oliver's shack. From here a path went east, crossed the railbed, and ended at the swamp. Just off the trail near the water was where Cadman had built his one-room, one-door, one-window, tarpaper home. Mr. Oliver got out, closed the door, and then leaned back in through the rear window. Holding the knife and beads in his palm, he said,

"Fellas, thanks again. When a'm gone, there's a bead for each a ya." He then went around to the driver's side and, laying his hand on Mr. Morracy's arm, said one more thank-you. Then he turned and disappeared into the brush. He would proudly wear the broken knife and beads dangling from a lace around his neck for the rest of his life.

Ted moved to the front, and Mr. Morracy made a three-point turn on the narrow road and headed back north to town. Along the way, he filled the boys in on his history with Cadman Oliver and told them the story of the Indian Graves. As they pulled up in front of Ted's house, Mr. Morracy concluded with, "So now you know pretty much all of it." In his recounting, he hadn't tried to make excuses for his shortcomings in the matter, and he admitted to being grateful for the opportunity to redeem his past failings. "There's not many second chances in life; take 'em when ya can" were his final words on the point.

With Ted's gear piled on the porch, Mrs. Samulski, who as yet knew almost nothing about what had actually gone on, allowed herself to gush with gratitude for Oscar's "bringing our boys home safe."

"Ya kin thank Cadman Oliver more than me. They been through a lot, Missus, make sure he gets some sleep," was all the shy man was able to manage. He then drove off to deliver the other boys home.

Over a bowl of leftover spaghetti, Ted gave his stunned mother and sister a brief sketch of events. He dozed off in the bath and then crawled into bed, where he slept through to Sunday breakfast. Zolly's experience was something similar. Unfortunately, Mr. Sweeny had taken his pay and gone on a binge after his Friday shift, and he didn't really sober up enough to find out what had happened to his son until Tuesday. But Buzzy's grandmother took good care of him, and Sunday night he slept over at Ted's, where, at supper, he was able to recount his version of the past five days.

⚘

Mr. Morracy had himself a very busy weekend. After dropping off the boys, he stopped to pick up a paper at Curley's Smoke Shop on Main Street. Word that something more than a fire had happened out at the old Herrod place was beginning to trickle back to town along with the returning firemen.

"Heard ennathin, Oska?" asked Curley Swenson as Mr. Morracy picked up his *Boston Globe*.

"Dunno," Oscar drawled, slipping a bit deeper into the local speech pattern. "Sumpthin' 'bout some boat from Pro-bition times sunk out-a Frenchman's Cove. Dickey Herrod and Gus Ouellette mixed up in it, someways," was all he needed to say to give the rumors a little more momentum.

By the time he got back to the marina, his earlier call to Tom Sesnick was already producing results. Several cars were parked in the lot, and boats that docked with him were out. It was a good thing he had ordered an extra gas delivery, as there was already someone waiting in the fueling bay. He spent the rest of the day pumping gas, collecting launching fees, and giving directions. He never got a chance to read his paper. By five o'clock, there were four boats buzzing around over the wreck. By seven, after supper, there were a dozen. Well after dark, there were still a few trying to see to the bottom with makeshift lights.

Two trucks managed to get down the old road to the shore of Frenchmen's Cove, and there would have been more if somebody in a passenger car hadn't tried to drive in and bottomed out. It took until past midnight for a tow truck to pull the car out. Someone managed to snag one of the slot-machine cases with a hook and brought it back to town to put on display, under lights, in his driveway. People from all over came to look at it.

Saturday started as an even bigger carnival. The town was humming with the news, and with the weekend off, people rose early to get out to the lake and Herrod's Farm. Reporters from the Worcester and Boston papers arrived, and members of a diving club from Providence made pests of themselves trying to rent the *Lady* as a dive boat. Ted's dad had to sit out on the front porch reading his paper to keep people from ringing the doorbell.

Generally speaking, police from the two states involved were caught off guard. The Mass "staties" took the investigation away from the town police, but they were unable to field divers or a boat to anchor out at the site, so they had to go back to Chief Stablocki, hat in hand, and ask him to come up with a couple of picket boats. On the Connecticut side, the burned-over farm attracted people from three states. Traffic snarled on the Windham Road as sightseers slowed to get a view of the crime scene. When someone found the few gutted slot machines and the single coin that the boys had overlooked at Frenchman's Cove, word spread that silver dollars were scattered all over. Another rumor spread that the police had set Herrod's fields on fire so they could find the coins more easily. Cars parked everywhere as people began walking in, looking for money on the ground. The old railbed got more foot traffic than it had seen in years. When the Connecticut police were finally able to cordon off most of the farmland, the path to where Dickey had died became a focus of attention. Some said that he had a sack of gold on him just before he died and had hidden it in the ledge along the trail—or maybe he threw it in the swamp as "a kinda offerin' to his dead motha." People were everywhere, and all sorts of rumors developed. Dozens of sightings of Gus were reported.

When the Massachusetts State Police finally got

professional divers in on Sunday, they pulled up nearly three hundred bottles of various liquors, and because the boys dumped most of the slot-machine carcasses in one spot, they brought those up too. On Monday, they looked over the wreck, trying to determine who its owner had been. The tiller that Buzzy had moved turned out to be the most important single clue. The divers were using the Breezy Point Marina as their base of operations, and as they unloaded their find that day, Mr. Morracy immediately recognized the tiller as his own work.

As a very young man, long before the marina was even a dream, Oscar Morracy had done modifications on an old lifeboat for a local entrepreneur by the name of Grant Keller. The major part of young Oscar's effort had been to install a motor and rudder, but significant effort was also devoted to muffling the boat's exhaust noise. Keller docked the boat at his big house on the town end of the lake and had it fitted with cushions and a canopy for cruises, though he rarely seemed to take it out for that purpose. When one day the boat wasn't there any more, Keller explained its disappearance by saying that he had sold it to a guy down on the Rhode Island coast, adding that he was looking for something better. Next season the *Lady of the Lake* arrived. It was impossible to know for sure if she had ever been used as a "rum runner," since Prohibition ended soon thereafter, but it was likely she'd made at least a few trips. Coincidental with the end of Prohibition, Grant Keller's fortunes began to decline. Eventually the house was sold for taxes. Oscar Morracy was able to present bills for various work and services rendered that, in rough calculation, offset the value of the *Lady*, so he got to keep the big speedboat that he already had in storage. Keller died in Florida a few years later.

"Well," mused Chief Stablocki, "Keller and Carl wouldn't be

the only ones in this town who made a buck off of Prohibition." It was true. Many small-town businessmen had gotten their first leg up during that era.

Mr. Morracy had to sit down to process it all. "So I'm the guy who set up that sunken boat out there for smugglin', and the *Lady* was bought with the bootlegger's money. And I never knew a thing. Well I'll be … Don't think I'll ever trust myself again," he said with a sense of total wonder. "It was right there under ma darn nose all the time, and here, like a fool, I'm imaginin' that old lifeboat chuggin' around in the Narragansett Bay ta this very day, and it's been sittin' right there on the bottom all the time, ha!"

On Wednesday, to everyone's excitement, a floatplane landed on South Pond, taxied around a bit, scared off a few boats, and then took off again. No one knew who was in it or where they came from. A couple of energetic reporters walked in, trying to find Cadman Oliver at his place. Mr. Morracy heard that Cadman saw them coming and ducked into the woods until they satisfied themselves with snapping pictures of the shack and went away. In another day, the police completed their investigation and left. They chained off the roads into Frenchman's Cove and the farm and dutifully posted "Keep Out" signs, but people immediately ignored those and went in anyway. The new rumor was that Carl had buried his money, so now they came with picks and shovels. The area around the charred foundations had so many holes dug in it that it looked like a bomb site. Others began to drag hooks and makeshift dredges across the sunken boat so that its outline was obliterated. No one, however, went near the base of the underwater ledge, and no one thought to question why so much of the cove had been swept clear.

In a week, school started. The papers had quoted police divers saying that they were amazed by the boys' resourcefulness and diving ability, so even the bullies and the snobs were impressed enough to give the three some respect. Mercifully, no English teacher assigned an essay on "What I Did on My Summer Vacation."

In a month, a coroner's hearing closed the case when it confirmed the police report that found a self-inflicted wound had killed Dickey Herrod. What had apparently happened was that, in his fury, Dickey pushed into the bushes holding the shotgun by its barrel. The safety was off, and the trigger snagged on a twig. The resulting shot caught him in the rib cage under his left arm. He had loaded the gun with buckshot, and pellets were found in his heart; he probably never knew what hit him. As for Gus, he was never seen again. He probably got out of town somehow—maybe on a northbound freight train, or he could have fled deep into the state forest and died of an infection, or stumbled off a cliff. It was a big place, and there were many areas where no one ever went. Some claimed that on full-moon nights in August, you could hear his voice moaning from the swamp.

As for the coins, it took a lawyer and a few months to get those back. The state of Massachusetts insisted that the coins and liquor were the product of illegal activity and refused to release them. The silver and all two hundred bottles of liquor were to be sold at a property auction. A young lawyer, Benno LaBoeuf, known locally as "LaBuff da lawya," took up the boys' case and made himself an enduring reputation as the clever fellow who could fight city hall. He managed to find a precedent in which recovered liquor was ruled the property of the finder as long as the taxes were paid on it. Judge Sumner, another local, used that ruling as reason enough to deliver a judgment that all the coins and half the proceeds from the sale of the liquor would go to Ted, Buzzy, and Zolly.

The silver was sold as a lot to a dealer, and the hooch brought a high price at auction. In the end, they each got about seven hundred dollars. For Ted and Zolly, that became the start of their college savings. The judge prevented Mr. Sweeny from drinking up Buzzy's share by putting it in trust until he was twenty-one.

All three boys finished high school. Ted went on to get his doctorate in archeology, studying Native American tribes of the Northeast. Zolly got an engineering degree and became a helicopter pilot in the army. Buzzy went to cooking school and worked most of his life as the head chef at the Hidden Valley Country Club near Boston. He became famous as the local expert on game cooking, and his venison dinners were legendary. Their friendship lasted all their lives, and all three stayed close to both Mr. Morracy and Cadman Oliver. No trip home for any of them was complete without a visit to the boathouse or to Cadman's shack in the woods.

For Buzzy, this connection with Cadman Oliver was crucial. Mr. Sweeny proceeded to drink himself to death in the years immediately following the boys' adventure, and each of those years became more difficult than the last. Buzzy spent many nights at the shack with the old man, who comforted him with patient listening and acceptance. He taught Buzzy everything he knew of field and stream. Eventually, he even began referring to Buzzy as his son. As for Cadman himself, his status in the community rose a little, though no one could make him quit the shack. His last years were good, even though his haunted loneliness never really left him.

Mr. Morracy's marina business grew slowly. His brother's Breezy Point Restaurant opened and struggled along. The story of the "Bootlegger's Trail" became part of the lake's history. The deaths in Herrod's Swamp became part of its mythology. In a few years, both strands of the story merged into the category of local color, repeated as anecdotes whenever the lake came up in conversation. When Oscar Morracy died in 1982, the *Lady*—the boat, that is—went to a museum in upstate New York, where it had been built. As for the other two "ladies of the lake," Theta Herrod and the mysterious figure beneath Frenchman's Cove, it would have to be said: they abide.

CHAPTER 14

1962

The telephone rang just after dawn as a gray October light filtered through thin drapes into the rented room where Ted Samulski slept. His mattress lay on the floor, and the shelf where the phone sat was no more than a pine board supported on cinderblocks. In truth, it was a comfortable mattress, and the blankets were warm. As he fumbled for the receiver, the index finger of his free hand probed at a crust in the corner of one eye. "'Lo," he said weakly. He ran his hand through his hair and stretched. When he heard the voice on the other end, he became alert. "Yah, oh, yah, yah. Okay, yah. Okay, yah ... about, about, about ... aaaah, an hour and a half, maybe a little more. You okay? Yah, I'll be there. Okay, see ya. I'm on my way." That was the sum total of his half of the conversation.

Fifteen minutes later, the engine of his VW microbus was

getting warm enough to put out heat as he rolled through the Mass Turnpike ticket booth at Exit 1 and followed the signs pointing west. He was twenty-two, living in Cambridge studying archeology, and he didn't get back home much. His department had been doing a lot of work out on Cape Cod. Now that it was going to become a national seashore, all of his summer and most of his weekends had been spent "East of America," as they say out on the cape. He drove within the speed limit for forty minutes and got off at Auburn, paid his toll, and headed south on Route 12 into Oxford, where he turned onto side roads in order to skirt Manchaug Lake and Slaterville. On this particular day, he didn't want to be recognized in his own hometown. As he drove, he thought about his father busy in the bakery and his mother asleep, and he regretted being so near and not stopping in to surprise them.

There was no straight route to his destination, so he picked his way along to a back road that paralleled the east side of the lake. He passed the old road down to Frenchman's Cove. After a while, he took an unmarked right off the paved road onto an old Civilian Conservation Corps trail, drove in a hundred yards, and stopped in a laurel thicket that screened his vehicle from view. He rummaged through the clutter in the back and came up with a coil of rope and the entrenching tool used on their camping trip many years before. *After all,* he mused, *what self-respecting archeologist would go anywhere without a shovel?* He locked up and set off down a trail that led south and west. There had been a frost, and the air had the clear, dry hardness of late fall. The trees were bare, and the seamless overcast sky lent an appropriately solemn light to the task he had before him.

After walking about two miles, he met Buzzy coming the other way. The young men quietly exchanged greetings, and then they headed back in the direction that Buzzy had come. In another mile, they came to a bit of open water that was the eastern shore of Herrod's Swamp. In the quiet shallows sat the old rowboat. It now had a five-horsepower outboard motor clamped to its stern. They climbed in and rowed a short distance to the opposite shore. Cadman Oliver's shack was just up ahead. Inside, his body lay on his narrow iron bedframe. Buzzy had skillfully stitched it into a canvas shroud, the result being that the corpse looked much like a mummy.

"When'd he go?" asked Ted.

"Yesterday, late," answered Buzzy. "He went quietly. There was some coughin'. It was the cigarettes got 'im." Cadman had indulged himself with tobacco in his later years, and he seemed never to be without a cigarette on his lip. Everyone who saw him remarked that the habit had taken a toll. Ted noticed for the first time how the drafty shack reeked of tobacco smoke. The smell had always been one with the man. Now that he was gone, the sour odor seemed to stand in for his presence.

Buzzy cut a few threads on the shroud and lifted a flap to expose the upper half of Cadman's body. The familiar face looked a bit more rutted and drawn, making its high cheekbones and broad forehead stand out. His long white hair lay loose on either side of his head. He wore his blue coat. His felt hat with the turkey quill was rolled and tucked into the waistband of his pants. With his arms crossed over his chest, his right hand grasped the broken stone blade and a rosary.

Buzzy held out his palm, with two shell beads cradled in it. "You got Zolly's address?" he asked.

Ted nodded yes. Zolly was on duty in Vietnam, but Ted was sure he could locate him.

"Send this to 'im, and tell 'im what we're doing," said Buzzy.

They folded the canvas back over, and Buzzy sewed its edges down snug. Ted went outside and began lashing together poles that Buzzy had prepared for a stretcher. When they had both finished, they carried the body out and tied it in, along with a large canvas tarp, a bucket, and the two shovels they had. With Buzzy in front, they grunted into their first lift and headed off south on a path that followed the west bank of the swamp.

Though Mr. Oliver had lost considerable weight, the extra gear brought the load up to what they figured was one-seventy, one-eighty. In the next mile and a half, they had ample opportunity to second-guess that estimate. For the last third of the portage, they left the path and struggled through the brush, being as careful as they could to minimize any sign of passage. Ted learned for the first time that stepping one foot directly in front of the other was not a particularly good way to walk if you happened to be balancing a heavy load. They came to a stop on a small rise above a boggy open area that expanded south for an acre. Along the far edge was a stream. To their left, open grassy ground sloped down to fringe the swamp. Just beyond the drip line of the trees, before the meadow grass got thick, was a narrow band that was as likely as anyplace to be good digging, free of stones and roots.

This was the place Cadman Oliver had picked for himself. In years past, they had walked out here with him many times, and invariably the old man would turn the conversation to how and where he wanted to be buried. It was a very important topic with him, and he had considered many places. This meadow, because of its view and because it was inside the boundaries of the state forest and unlikely to ever be developed, was where he wanted to be. They set the body down and carefully cleared the top layer of leaves from what they judged to be the best spot. They then scratched out a three-by-six rectangle on the dark earth and spread the tarp at its uphill edge.

Digging was slow but went well. They encountered no

large obstructions that couldn't be moved, and in a little over three hours they had a six-by-three-by-six-foot-deep hole with fairly straight sides and a flat bottom. Toward the end of their digging, the trench was too small to hold both of them and too deep to even swing a loaded shovel, so they took turns with the stubby entrenching tool, filling the bucket and passing it out to the man on the surface, who added its contents to the growing pile on the tarp. There was somehow comfort in the fact that the ground was dry all the way down.

With the hole finished, they took time to eat. Ted had gotten two anemic-looking tuna sandwiches at a turnpike plaza, but Buzzy trumped him with a couple of stew burgers from Pap's Diner in town. "Got 'em yesterday," he said. "Cadman loved 'em, but obviously ..." he trailed off.

"Dead man's food?" said Ted. "I didn't need ta know that."

"Go on," grinned Buzzy. "He would want us ta have 'em. You know how he hated to waste food."

They walked to the stream and washed their hands, and then sat near Cadman to eat. On the way out of his place in Cambridge, Ted had grabbed a leather wineskin he had gotten in Spain and filled it with some jug wine. In the end, they ate all four sandwiches, washing them down with swallows of the cheap wine.

When they finished, their mood grew serious again. They moved the stretcher next to the hole, and Ted jumped down inside. Buzzy shifted the body over, and taking the weight on his shoulders, Ted lowered it down gently. He was grateful that the heavy canvas kept him from feeling the flesh and bones of the body inside. The hole was ample for the small package, and it laid out easily. After Ted got a hand up from Buzzy, they both looked down for several minutes, thinking their good-byes. Buzzy began to sob. When his crying tapered off, Ted reached into the game pouch of his vest and pulled out three

Dutch Masters panatelas that he had bought some time ago for just this moment. Buzzy regained himself and smiled broadly as Ted tossed them into the grave. Next, Ted lowered in the wineskin by its strap and let it drop near Cadman's shoulder. "For the journey," he said.

With his sheath knife, Buzzy cut the long poles in half. Those and the other stretcher components went in beside the body. Filling in the hole, of course, was much faster than digging it. At first they put in only soil, and then they began to mix in stones. When it was all back in place, there was a slight mound, and it took a good deal of foot stomping and pounding with shovel blades to ram the earth back to its original contours. Satisfied, they found some fallen branches and used them to rake leaves back over the spot. As they were fussing with these finishing touches, it occurred to Ted that this was the second time that his well-worn little shovel had dug a secret hole. He puzzled on that for a moment but could come up with no reason except that the thing was just damn handy.

They checked around for anything they might have left and exited by an alternate route. Fortunately for them, it would rain hard that night, and the soaked leaves would quickly settle back into an even mat. Back at the shack, they rinsed the shovel and bucket that belonged to Cadman, putting the items back in place. Ted took the tarp, the rope, and his shovel with him. There was nothing else to do. Buzzy rowed him back across the swamp, and they parted as Ted headed to his vehicle. Back in Boston that night, he slept soundly.

>~

For Buzzy's part, he motored the length of the lake back to

the town dock, where he still kept the boat. He had secretly made his call to Ted from the marina's new outside pay phone. On this pass, he stopped to inform Mr. Morracy of his friend's death. In a few days, Buzzy reported Cadman missing. Some search parties were organized, but they found nothing. After that, Cadman Oliver's story became part of town history. He would forever be assigned the role of "the last of the full-blooded Nipmuck," and his ghost joined the others that wandered Herrod's Swamp.

〜

A week later, after a letter had been written and a single shell bead mailed to a military post-office address in Saigon, Ted was proctoring an exam, part of the job associated with his fellowship. As he looked out over the room full of nodding heads and scratching pencils, he found himself absentmindedly fingering the bead that hung around his neck, and he wondered how many of these history majors would ever handle material from an excavation. He asked himself how many might become archeologists out in the field on a dig. And he wondered if any of them would ever know what it felt like to put something sacred back into the ground.

CHAPTER 15

2004

A quick snap of the forearm and a well-timed release let the translucent line whir out through the eyelets of Professor Ted Samulski's spinning rod. The shiny brass lure glinted in the ten o'clock sun as it arched through the air and hit the water, fifty feet away, with a delicate but satisfying plunk. He worked the crank on the reel one turn to click over the bail and then let the little gold fish sink a bit before he began to bring it in. There was little chance of catching anything at this time of day out in front of Frenchman's Cove, but fishing was a good cover for his meditation. He had occasionally used the ploy to get out here to think.

In the summer of '55, the three boys had used the same ruse to cover their diving to check out the ledge. They were surprised by how much silt they had managed to push out of the cove, and how natural the bottom looked. He and Buzzy had come out here to talk when they got the news that Captain Zoltan Dracut was missing in action in Vietnam.

They had also made one final outing in the *Lady of the Lake* when Mr. Morracy died in '82. And Ted had come out today to wrestle with his conscience and ponder the future. At the moment, there was much at stake in his life. In the years since grad school, Ted had made a name for himself pioneering underwater archeology in these freshwater lakes. With all the damming that had gone on during the Industrial Revolution, many Native American sites were now underwater. He had been among the first to locate flooded campgrounds, shell middens, and flint tailings in many New England lakes. In all his work, however, he had never seen a blade anything like the one that Cadman Oliver carried in plain view around his neck. The burial it came from must certainly go back to the earliest days of habitation, when ancient hunter-gatherers were following the edge of the retreating glaciers north and the environment slowly changed from arctic grasses to temperate forest. A time long before the tribes we know had named themselves. A time we could only access though its artifacts. The knife was by far the oldest local object he had ever seen. The "discovery" of a Paleo-Indian site in Mashpaug Lake would push back the date of the area's earliest culture and add much to knowledge in the field. There was little doubt it would be a major find, a valuable new page in history. It could also cinch his bid for chairmanship of the archeology department at U Mass and bring in funding for future work. A find like that was once-in-a-lifetime. It could be the crowning achievement of his career and assure his enduring reputation. Looking over to the shore of the cove, where lakefront houses were now being built, he could easily rationalize that someone might eventually stumble onto it. He told himself that his work would preserve the artifacts. The knowledge could benefit everyone. History would be served. In time, the rising acidity of the lake water would probably dissolve the bones anyway. Heck, he might get the tribes at the casinos down in Ledyard to fund such a spectacular project.

He made a few more casts as his canoe drifted south with the breeze, and then he pulled out the paddle and headed toward Skunk Island. He didn't land there but passed close enough to note how little it had changed. The pines were a bit taller and shaggier, but the Skunk's Nose sat as it always had—ponderous and dark, drinking in the sun. Connecticut had expanded the state forest to take in most of the swamp and the island; thankfully, it would never be built on. At Lakeside, the bushes were thinner than he recalled, and he had little trouble pulling his light boat up and chaining it to a tree. He hid his gear a few paces off the trail before heading for Herrod's Farm. The trail toward the trolley bed was now well worn and littered, but every step of the way still had enough familiarity to stir memories. When he reached the old rail line, he wasn't surprised to see that off-road vehicles and snowmobiles had almost turned it into a road. There was currently talk in the two towns, Windham and Slaterville, about having the path graded into a bicycle and walking trail.

The barway was gone, rotted to oblivion, but stone walls still led toward the farm. When Dickey died, there was no one to inherit the place, and it had been in the care of the town of Windham ever since. There wasn't much to do but mow the fields once or twice a year, and for that small effort the land now had a groomed park-like look. The road in had been paved, and there were a couple of picnic tables, a barbecue grill, and a trash can in the flat spot between the foundations of the house and barn. As he passed between the two filled-in holes, he was amused to see that there was fresh digging around the place. *Likely some fourteen-year-old boys, looking for buried treasure,* he thought. He proceeded up the access road to Route 173 and walked the edge of the pavement to the spot where they had let Cadman Oliver off those many years ago. The way in to the shack was almost overgrown, and there was nothing left of the structure but the four stacks of flat stones that had been its foundation. The shack's demise had been swift. Within a year of Cadman's death, it was stripped of the little it had contained, and then some vandal had set it on fire. If you scrubbed through the leaves, bits of charred wood and rusty nails could still be found.

The next leg of his walk took Ted to Cadman's grave. He couldn't stop himself from traveling part of the way by placing one foot in front of the other, but the objective scientist in him chastised his inner romantic for trying to recapture a moment of youthful foolishness. The place had changed little. In the mysterious way that natural meadows have of persisting, the grassy center remained open, and the stream still kept its bed moist with drainage from the sloping ground. The grave was undetectable, though Ted knew exactly where it was. He had been out here a few times over the years.

Ted sat for several hours thinking and eating his lunch. Finally, in midafternoon, he rose and walked back through the woods to a nearby stone wall, where he selected a flat, rounded stone about the size of a small hubcap and carried it back to the grave. From the pocket of his vest he pulled a well-used garden trowel that was currently his favorite excavation tool, and he set to work digging a sloping pit into which he neatly fit the rock so that it protruded at a low angle. He scattered the extra soil and raked the leaves back into place. There was now a marker that would go unnoticed by the casual onlooker, but if need be he could direct someone to the spot. He then produced three cigars, removed their cellophane wrappings, and, crumbling the tobacco between his palms, sprinkled it over the grave.

All the knowledge and experience of a lifetime as an

archeologist didn't make his dilemma any less sharp. *Surely, he thought, history would benefit by knowing what lay beneath Frenchman's Cove, but history is a device for the living. What about the wishes of the dead? Aren't we all diminished if we disregard those?*

As he walked away, he paid close attention to his feet as they rose and fell against the earth.

CPSIA information can be obtained at www.ICGtesting.com
Printed in the USA
BVOW020823020413

317006BV00001BA/5/P